CHANGING TIMES

ff

CHANGING TIMES

Tim Kennemore

faber and faber
LONDON · BOSTON

First published in 1984
by Faber and Faber Limited
3 Queen Square London WC1N 3AU

Typeset by Set Fair Ltd
Printed in Great Britain by
The Thetford Press Ltd Thetford Norfolk
All rights reserved

British Library Cataloguing in Publication Data

Kennemore, Tim
Changing times.
I. Title
823'.914 [J]   PZ7
ISBN 0-571-13285-5

ONE

An enormous parcel had arrived for Victoria. She had never seen anything like it. Big enough to hold two large television sets, three at a pinch, or a jukebox, a pinball machine, maybe a baby elephant. There was a label on it which said 'To Rosemary', but this could not be helped. Eagerly she tore at the wrapping, gouging viciously with her fingernails. How fortunate that her parents were out at the bridge club, or her mother might try to claim it, although she was called Pat. Nobody was to be trusted. And now the wrapping was all on the floor, and the box beginning to come open, to reveal its delicious secret. And then the alarm clock screamed into Victoria's ear, waking her so rudely, and at such a frustrating moment, that in her fury she grabbed it and hurled it across the room. It hit the wardrobe, produced a surprised-sounding clunk, and fell stone dead to the floor.

Victoria was very pleased by this. She should have done it years ago. A growing girl needed her sleep. She rolled over, and buried her head under the duvet.

"Victoria, what was that awful noise?" said her mother, poking her tousled, bleary, early-morning head around the door. "Have you . . . oh, what the hell have you done to the clock? Who do you think's going to pay to have that mended? For God's sake, Victoria, if you can't . . ." There was a pause. "Happy birthday, Victoria."

7

Victoria, who had been paying little attention up to that point, suddenly began to take an interest in the day. Yes, so it was. March the tenth, and she was fifteen. She might as well get up; there would be presents. This brought back the dream — obviously her dreaming-self had remembered. She sat up and swung her legs to the floor.

"You're getting up, then," said her mother, hovering there in her dressing-gown as if to witness a rare phenomenon. Normally it took the alarm and at least three good shouts before Victoria would stir. "Happy birthday," she said again. Victoria grunted in acknowledgement and wandered out to the bathroom, where she stared at her face in the mirror for quite some time, and from several different angles, before washing it. She heard her father stomp sleepily out of his room and curse at finding the bathroom occupied, so she decided to clean her teeth for once, most meticulously, paying enormous attention to every little crevice with a toothpaste guaranteed to reduce decay by sixty per cent.

"Victoria, will you get moving!" roared her father, who was hopping around in agony by this time. It was very gratifying. She unlocked the door and swept past him, an offended expression on her face. A girl must take care of her teeth. There were still another forty per cent of decay to be contended with.

She had another good look at herself in her wardrobe mirror while she dressed. This one was full length: much more satisfying. How lucky that the clock had hit the other side of the wardrobe. There was little that interested Victoria quite as much as her own reflection. She was a doll-like creature, her hair long and blonde, her face pink and white, her whole appearance so fragile, so innocent that once at Junior School she'd got clean away with cracking Martin Bradshaw's head open on a radiator; the teacher couldn't believe her capable of such an act. The rest of the class had been most severely lectured for telling such lies, and on the cowardice of failing to own up, while Victoria happily eyed the splodges of blood on the wall behind the pipes. Fifteen, thought Victoria, brushing her golden hair with loving care. A *very* difficult age.

Over in the kitchen the opening salvoes had been fired and the battle was well under way.

"Oh, very clever! Yes! So you took the double out! It was going for eleven hundred, that's *eleven hundred*, Pat, and you took it out! You *liked* them so much that you decided to give them a present of our money! I've told you before: if I double . . . "

"Well, hello," said Victoria, sitting down.

"Look, Simon, could we leave this for later?" said her mother, whose face had gone all pink and pinched with fury. "It is Victoria's birthday, for God's sake."

"Oh, don't mind me," said Victoria, helping herself to cornflakes. "You just go ahead and work out whose fault it was. I mean, I have a birthday every single year, it's nothing special. It's obviously a lot more important that Mum didn't want eleven hundred . . ."

"That's not true!" shouted her mother, while her father gave Victoria a look that said, very clever, you little stirrer. "It was going two off, three at most, three with expert defence which is highly unlikely with your father playing, so two off, that's five hundred, Simon, watch my lips, *five* — much better to take the rubber . . ."

Thursday mornings were always like this. Every Wednesday night they played partnership rubber bridge at the club; they played together all evening, and every week they swore that they would never, no, not at *gunpoint* would they play with the other again. Her father was always the more rancorous of the two. His wife's play, he would claim, was taking years off his life. It made him want to weep. He had married a certifiable lunatic, unfit to hold thirteen cards. It was fortunate that this partnership bridge occurred only once a week. On other nights they played with a succession of random partners, but never with each other. This led to breakfast-table acrimony of quite a different nature; both of them would be railing away about the total idiocy of the morons they had been landed with, each one of whom should have been strangled at birth out of kindness to its mother . . . neither listening to a word that the other said. Only Thursdays were murderous. Every bid by her mother must be scorned by her father, the play of every hand torn apart, the blame apportioned down to a fraction of a per cent.

"I thought it was Victoria's birthday," said Mr Hadley

9

virtuously, as his wife drew breath. "Shouldn't she have her presents now?"

"Oh . . . yes, of course." A pile of parcels was fetched from her parents' bedroom. "And all these cards in the post, Victoria. You've done very well, this year."

"Good," said Victoria, putting her cornflakes bowl aside and deliberately cutting a sausage into five pieces of identical length, before turning her attention to the presents. First she opened the cards — all from seldom-seen relations. Gran, of course, had sent a present — a little locket on a chain. Half of the locket was empty, for a photo, and the other half held a tiny oval mirror. Victoria fastened it round her neck. A girl could never have too many mirrors. Then her parents' parcels. A blue dress; a pen, and writing paper with envelopes to match; blue shoes to go with the dress; eye shadow in three smoky shades; a five pound book token; one of those cute little Walkman stereos.

"Thank you," said Victoria. "You're so kind. Thank you very much. Very nice things." In vain her parents waited for further comment, for Victoria to show signs of trying on the dress, to test the stereo, to slip on the shoes.

"Well — what do you think of the dress?" asked her mother. "I thought it would suit you down to the ground."

"Down to the knees, actually," was her father's contribution, his once-yearly birthday effort at riotous family merriment.

"It's a lovely dress," Victoria said. "They're all lovely things. Would you pass the toast?"

"Yes, yes, let's have toast," said her father, as if toast were the one thing that might save the situation. "Toast!"

"And still your present from Joe and Eileen to come," said Mrs Hadley. These were Victoria's aunt and uncle. It had long been the custom that Victoria should, each year, choose her own present from their shop. "What will you do — go on the bus after school?"

"Yes, I should think so. Yes, I will."

"I hope it won't be knives again this year, Victoria."

"No, not knives," said Victoria, adding vaguely: "I was hoping for an assegai." There was a silence, and then her mother said, in rather strained tones:

"Well, I shan't be going to the club tonight, Victoria. It's your father's teaching night, so of course he has to go, but I'll stay behind . . ."

Victoria knew all about teaching at the bridge club; it had been explained to her. Her father would, for one hour precisely, supervise four beginners of fantastic imbecility. The rest of the evening he'd be doing just what he did all the other evenings, playing rubber bridge, playing cards for money.

". . . on your birthday," her mother said, still rambling away. "Unless, of course, you've got other plans for tonight?" Victoria sensed a rising note of hope in this last sentence. "Perhaps you'll be staying with Joe and Eileen, as you don't see them that often . . ."

"What on earth would I want to stay there for?"

"Well, I don't know . . . or perhaps you want to do something with Daniel."

"I've told you enough times, Daniel's cruddy father won't let me see him during the week. Not until his cruddy A levels are over."

"I'm sorry, yes, I forgot. I suppose he is acting for the best — though Daniel's so clever, somehow it's hard to picture him failing."

"He'd get three A's if he slept from now till June," said Victoria. "And his father knows that. It's just any excuse to keep his family under lock and key. I can't even ring up, in case I take Daniel's mind off a theorem."

"Yes . . . Mr Priestley does sound rather a difficult man. Over-strict."

"He's a revolting disgusting decomposing tail-end of a toad's turd," said Victoria. "He stinks!" Another silence. "So, the answer is, no, I've got absolutely nothing planned for tonight at all. Just another regular boring evening." She stood up and pushed her chair in. "And now I'd better get going."

"I thought she might have said something about the stereo," Mrs Hadley muttered as her daughter disappeared into her room with the presents.

"Toad's turd," said Mr Hadley, chuckling to himself. "No bridge for you tonight then, Pat," he added maliciously.

"There's a documentary on BBC2," Mrs Hadley said stiffly, "about Battersea Dogs' Home." She drained her coffee, which would be the first of many that day, and shouted: "Victoria! It's half past eight already."

Victoria picked up the yellow plastic carrier which was currently the fashionable thing for carrying schoolbooks, straightened the First World War German officer's bayonet which hung on her wall, and gave her reflection one last admiring glance.

The Hadleys lived in West Hampstead, in a house divided into three flats; theirs was the middle one, on the first floor. Victoria liked it well enough. Her bedroom was big, bigger than at their old place in Ladbroke Grove, and that was really what mattered. The rest of the flat was a disgusting mess, thanks to her mother's ideas about cleaning, which were, apparently, that you sat back and waited for something to happen. But Victoria rarely left her own room. It was lucky that her school, St. Catherine's, was only five minutes' walk away. She was far too lazy to walk more than a quarter of a mile, and too impatient to endure waiting for a bus.

My birthday, she thought, trying to look a bit special as she strutted along, exactly in the middle of the pavement so as to cause maximum inconvenience to those walking the other way. It felt exactly like any other day. She could remember a time when a birthday had made her feel like the queen of the world. How important eight years old had felt, after a whole year of being seven. But it wasn't like that any more — it hadn't been for years, now. That was what growing up did for you. And Christmas! Victoria had got so worked up about Christmas when she was little — she'd gone potty with anticipation. These days Christmas was a positive nightmare of boredom. She was the wrong age for Christmas. She was the wrong age for everything.

St. Catherine's was considered by the local parents to be a very good Comprehensive. This meant that, what with it being single-sex, and having school uniform, streaming, impressive exam results and a general lack of trendy subjects like 'Community Studies', if you didn't think about it too much you could forget that it was a Comprehensive at all.

Victoria turned in at the main gate and set about finding her particular good friend Lesley, who should have been there to meet her, but there you were, nobody was to be relied on. Eventually she tracked her down in the bicycle sheds, squatting on the ground and feverishly scribbling in her Geography exercise book, under a drawing which might have been the North East Industrial Region, but with a few names changed could probably have passed equally well as a diagram of the human stomach, liver, pancreas and duodenum.

"Vic, hi, happy birthday, look at this garbage, I forgot to take it home last night, had to sneak in just now and get it, and you try drawing a map with nothing but your knees to lean on."

"You've left off Durham, or is it the gall bladder?" said Victoria, picking up Lesley's bag (yellow, plastic) and rifling through the contents. "Ah, here we are." She extracted a parcel and a card.

"Oh, get off that!" said Lesley, finding the spot where Durham should go, or so she hoped, and deciding not to ask about the gall bladder. "That'll have to do. Oh, go on then, open it."

"Good, good, chocolates," said Victoria, tearing the box open and cramming three soft-centres into her mouth. "Here, you take a few and then I'm hiding them. I don't mind Soph and Ally having one but I'm not passing them round the rest of those boring cows." Thus dismissing the remainder of form IVA, she stowed the chocolates safely away.

Victoria had a theory that the ideal friend for a pretty girl was someone who was also pretty, but in a quite different way. You drew attention to each other, but remained unchallenged in your own particular field. Lesley Aspinall, though she had been chosen on the basis of character, not looks, fitted the bill; she was good-looking in a sturdy, dark, healthy, beaming sort of way. They had an alliance with another couple, Sophie Priestley and Alison Betts, a good arrangement for all concerned, for if you had just the one special friend and she was off sick you were on your own for the day. IVA were very cliquey.

The bell rang; all the little knots and gaggles began to drift towards the school building. "What d'you get from your parents?" asked Lesley, scrambling undaintily to her feet. Victoria recited the list. "Blimey," said Lesley, who had four brothers — "there's a lot to be said for being an only child. Feel like swopping places?"

"I'll think about it," said Victoria, who had certainly never felt like anything of the sort. She had met the brothers. "Don't ring us, we'll ring you."

"Mind you, they can't have been losing too much at their bridge game."

Victoria snorted. "Losing? They win. My father's one of the best players in the club. Last night they won sixty-one points playing together, that's fifteen pounds twenty-five *each*, and they were blasting away this morning like they'd have to remortgage the flat."

"That must get so boring, especially if you don't understand the game."

"Of course it's boring, it's all they can talk about, four spades doubled going one off, thank you *very* much Pat, why can't you finesse like a human being. . ."

"How often do they play, then?"

"Mondays, Wednesdays, Thursdays, they both go. Tuesdays and Fridays my mother generally stays home for the sake of her conscience. Weekends vary. Usually they both play Sunday afternoon and my father stays on for the evening."

"Blimey," Lesley said again, for she hadn't realized it was anything like that bad; and as the second bell went and they flopped down at their desks, she decided that, all in all, she was quite glad to be herself.

TWO

Joe's and Eileen's shop wasn't a bad place; it was quite enjoyable poking around there, if you were left to yourself to get on with it. Victoria's father called it an antique shop, her mother a junk shop, from which it was not difficult to guess whose brother Uncle Joe was. As far as Victoria could make out, it was a bit of both, but with junk probably predominating. Still, it was a good shop for choosing a present. Imagine what might have happened if they'd owned a grocery — "Thank you for the lovely Bird's Eye cod in sauce, Auntie" — or an electrician's — "square pin adaptors *again*, Victoria?" Victoria smiled secretly at herself in a rather splendid pub mirror, which would look very good on her bedroom wall.

"How are you doing out there?" called Uncle Joe, who was pottering around in the back.

"Thinking," said Victoria. It seemed that assegais were in short supply in Swiss Cottage, and although she'd seen the cutest little Italian dagger in one of the boxes, she might well go for the mirror. But there was no hurry. In earlier years her mother had accompanied her and supervised her choices, and almost every time something had caught Victoria's eye her mother would hiss: "No, that's much too expensive" — until once Victoria had retorted: "How do you know? It isn't your shop" — at which point her mother had slapped her, and a wonderful birthday *that* had been. "Let her have whatever she'd like," Uncle Joe would say, but somehow she always ended up with what her mother wanted her to have.

And so for the past few years she had insisted on coming alone.

15

On the first occasion she had gone home with a set of three little knives, superbly lethal-looking, and originating from Burma. Such was her mother's disapproval that the next year, when she was fourteen, she had chosen the First World War bayonet. But perhaps another knife would be a bit boring — predictable, even. Probably the mirror, then, unless she saw something really special. There was still one corner to be investigated. And that was when she saw the clock.

It wasn't particularly beautiful, but it had character. It was something like an amputated cuckoo clock with all the twee bits removed; nine or ten inches high, made of carved wood with a roof-like peak along the middle of the top surface. The dial was only a couple of inches in diameter, with little white figures raised on the wood and delicate white hands, fixed at nine twenty-four, for the clock wasn't going. Victoria picked it up, found a key in the bottom and twisted it; there was a satisfying winding noise, and the clock began to tick.

Underneath the main dial was another, smaller one for setting the alarm, and this — now this *was* unusual — was numbered from one to twenty-four. A twenty-four hour alarm, so that if you wanted to set it for seven in the morning you could do precisely that, could do it at six o'clock the night before, without the thing going off an hour later. And she had just broken her alarm clock, and this one was so much more interesting. And — she had only just noticed this — the little alarm hand was pointing straight to the number fifteen, the age that Victoria had reached this very day. Perhaps . . .

"Uncle Joe," she called, "I think I've found something. I'd rather like this clock, unless, you know, unless it's worth a fortune or something . . ."

"That thing!" Her uncle came through and looked at the clock with great disdain. "It doesn't go."

"It does! I wound it. It's going now."

"You wait," said her uncle, and even as he said it the ticking died away, and the clock stopped. It had moved on to nine twenty-five. "It goes for a minute and then it stops. Every time. Don't bother with it, love. I'm not even going to try and have it fixed, not worth my while, nobody's going to want a daft little box

16

like that when I've got all these good clocks here. You want a clock? How about this one, predicts the weather as well, stick it on the wall and it'll last you for years . . ."

"No," said Victoria, somewhat taken aback by the depth of her disappointment. "It was this one that I liked." And then in a flash of delight she realized that it didn't matter — it didn't matter that the clock didn't go, it made it even better. "No, this clock is what I want. Clocks that don't work are the best clocks." She would walk in with the clock and her mother would say: "Oh Victoria, what a very sensible thing to get a new clock when you've broken the old one," and Victoria would say, ha ha, this one doesn't work either. "Time is a shackle," said Victoria, rising to her feet. "May I have it then, please?"

"Well, of course you can have it if you like it so much, if you want it as an ornament, sort of thing, I suppose it might look quite attractive . . . But, Vic, it doesn't seem like we've given you a real present, not when it was something we were throwing out. Tell you what. You take the clock as a favour to me, to save me getting rid of it, and have the mirror as your present. How about that?"

"All right," said Victoria, never one to refuse a good offer, and then she went up to the flat above the shop where Auntie Eileen had a birthday tea ready for her, leaving her uncle to wrap her new possessions.

Victoria always behaved nicely when she visited her aunt and uncle; she saw no point in doing otherwise. She only saw them a few times a year, and Auntie Eileen was a fantastic cook, which was not an asset to be trifled with.

So she answered all their questions politely; that's right, two O Levels she was doing this year, and the rest next, and, yes, she still wanted to do Biology at university, and her nice friend Lesley was just fine, and yes she was still with that clever boyfriend, clever *and* good-looking, you could do well there, Victoria — and she could sense a slight amusement, that they thought she was too young, that at her age having a boyfriend was rather sweet, but not to be taken seriously. Well, let them think what they liked — the first priority was to consume as much food as possible, which wasn't easy with all this talking. And all the time she was

17

forming a plan. So her mother had condescended to stay home tonight, had she? Well, right, she could stay there on her own, and see what it was like. When Uncle Joe said: "I'll run you home, love, you don't want to be lugging all those things on the bus," she said thanks, but she was going round to Lesley's to watch Top of the Pops, and could he run her there instead?

Lesley was very pleased to see Victoria. "I was so bored," she said, hustling her upstairs to her bedroom. Lesley had a little box of a room, but at least, being the only girl, she had it to herself. Victoria did not often visit — the brothers were too big, too loud and too numerous for her taste. They thought her a proper stuck-up little brat, and made this clear.

They spent the next couple of hours doing their homework, which was always so much easier, and more fun, when there were two of you, and afterwards, on her way out, Victoria managed to look so helpless with her great heavy parcels, *and* her school bag, that Mr Aspinall, like Uncle Joe before him, said that she couldn't possibly carry all that on her own, he'd give her a lift. Which was very acceptable. Victoria smiled to herself as she unlocked the front door of the house; it was past nine thirty, and a fine evening her mother would have had all on her own. She carried on smiling all the way up the stairs to the front door of their flat, until she opened it, found no lights on, a note in the kitchen, and nobody in. The note said:

Rang Joe — he said you'd gone on to L's so have decided to go to club for a few hours after all. Stew in oven — back eleven thirty — M.

"You rotten old cow!" shouted Victoria. "I hate you!" And if the Wilsons upstairs heard, so much the better. Well, she'd get back at her. She wouldn't eat that stinking stew for a start. And what else? . . .yes. There was a shop open just a few minutes away. She ran back down the stairs, banged the door loudly to wake the Shaws' baby, and charged off down the road to the general store, where she bought a packet of ten cigarettes. Fortunately they weren't fussy about whether you were over sixteen. Back in the flat, feeling much better now that she had a new plan of action, she closed all the windows, switched the TV on, settled down in her father's armchair with a bowl of Rice Krispies, two bags of crisps and an individual apple pie, and lit the first cigarette. This was horrible. You had to suck the thing, and it made her feel choky and smoky and revolting, but it had to be done. Then she stood it carefully in the ashtray, and left it to burn itself down. By the time she'd got through ten of them there'd be the most fantastic fuggy haze of smoke in the room, and her parents would absolutely do their nuts. She'd had this idea in reserve for some time, saving it up for the right occasion.

She watched the documentary on Battersea Dogs' Home, which convinced her that none of her parents' presents had been what she wanted. She wanted a dog, a lovely floppy shaggy dog, and typically they had denied it to her. She was just thinking what she would have called the dog, and was nearing the end of the sixth cigarette, when the telephone rang. Probably her mother to check that she was all right, and had she enjoyed the stew? Victoria knew you could always get someone by rejecting their food. "Yes?" she snarled, as money clicked into a slot, cutting off the pips.

"Victoria, is that you?" Daniel sounded considerably taken aback by this reception.

"Hello! Of course it's me."

"It didn't sound like you."

"I didn't think it was you," said Victoria, and adding: "Hang on a sec," fetched the ashtray and smouldering cigarette so that she could keep an eye on them. She didn't want a fire. "I'm back. Where are you?"

"Walking the dog," said Daniel. "Good idea isn't it? I don't know why I haven't thought of it before. I'll do it every night, now, and then I can ring you every night. Well, happy birthday. What have you been doing this week, then?"

"Nothing much," said Victoria. "Been round to my aunt's and to Lesley's tonight, and that's all really. We're getting lots of homework as well, you know."

"Oh. I mean, you haven't been going out anywhere, then."

"Honestly, Daniel, what are you after? You don't think I'm seeing someone else behind your back, do you?"

"That would be a terrible thing to do, Victoria," said Daniel.

19

"I don't thing I could ever trust anybody again."

"It doesn't sound as if you trust me now," said Victoria, rather crossly; how had the conversation taken such a stupid turn? "Oh Daniel, it's so good to hear your voice. When can I see you?"

"Well, I've got something for you — I thought I'd bring it round on Saturday. Will that be all right, Saturday?"

"Of course it will. Oh, and Daniel, you haven't got a little picture of yourself, have you? I mean really small, about one inch high, and sort of oval."

"Oh well, of course, I carry fourteen on me at all times," said Daniel. "Look you'll have to tell me on Saturday what all that's about. I can't stop, my father might guess what I'm doing, and that would be the end of it. What's the time?"

"Nearly quarter to eleven."

"I don't believe it. Must go. Bye then."

"Bye," said Victoria, hanging up with a rather cut-off sort of feeling. She did so wish that Friday might disappear; that she could move straight on to Saturday. She liked Daniel so very much. She could tell him absolutely anything.

Victoria had had one boyfriend before Daniel, if you could call it that. Keith Bellamy was his name, and she had only taken up with him on the principle that anything was better than nothing. Keith Bellamy was very nearly nothing. He kept guppies. That was all he could talk about: guppies and Tottenham Hotspur. Victoria knew she'd ditch him quicker than a rancid raspberry the moment something better came along.

She had much preferred to spend her time with Lesley, Sophie and Alison, discussing things of greater interest than Glenn Hoddle and guppies, which covered just about everything. The four of them had met regularly all through the previous summer, at Victoria's place or Alison's, seldom Lesley's because of the shortage of space, and never Sophie's because her father was potty. So potty was Mr Priestley that he wouldn't allow his daughter to be out after half past eight, not even at a friend's house — what's more, she had to be collected and escorted home. And so this boy had started to appear, a boy of seventeen or so with Sophie's dark hair and eyes, and a wistful, sad, spaniel face.

Victoria hadn't noticed him particularly at first, except to

20

think "so that's what Sophie's brother looks like" and "doesn't he ever smile?". After a while, though, she caught him looking at her out of the corner of his eye, as he stood there bashfully, silently, waiting for Sophie to get ready. Almost without being aware of it, she began to look forward to his arrival. She began to think that there were, after all, more attractive things to do with a face than to stretch it into a daft grin. She started to take a great interest in Sophie, whom she had previously liked the least of the other three. Daniel looked at her more and more. Keith Bellamy was given a very sharp elbow.

And nothing happened. Victoria thought she would go mad with the frustration of it. She was pretty — Sophie must have told him she was clever — she had smiled at him often enough — what was the matter with him? Until one day Sophie said to her:

"I wish you'd say something to my brother. He's dying to talk to you, only he's too shy to open his mouth."

Honestly, thought Victoria, I can't ask *him* out, for God's sake. Although this was quite wrong, and girls should be able to do anything boys could, unfortunately society hadn't moved that far forward yet, not amongst their circle anyway. She managed to get the gist of this over to Sophie, along with the impression that whilst it was all a considerable surprise to her, she was not unwilling. Sophie looked rather depressed about the whole thing, but then Sophie always did look depressed. It seemed to be a family trait.

And lo and behold, the very next day as she walked through the gates after school there he stood, the picture of awkwardness, shuffling his feet and looking as if he'd rather be on Mars. A group of third years were observing him with interest. But, against all the odds, he managed to say, quite clearly: "Am I walking you home, then?" with typical Priestley diffidence, and staring at a point on the pavement some yards behind her left foot. His voice, though, was deep and rich, a fantastic voice after Keith's little fishy squeakings, and he stood there looking so much like a floppy spaniel that has been kicked regularly and expects to be kicked again that she felt an absurd urge to pat him on the head.

Sometimes she still felt that way. He seemed to need so much

21

reassurance. This was because he was insecure, and unsure of himself. Victoria knew this from the magazines she read, which told you all there was to know about boys. They all had tremendous problems with their egos. Well, knowing that she wanted a picture of him to carry round in her locket ought to reassure him no end. She must write to Gran and thank her. Gran was the best person in her entire lousy family. But first, back to business; there were still four cigarettes to deal with.

But her initial rage had worn off now, and the last cigarettes didn't give her the pleasure that the first few had. Perhaps it hadn't been worth it — it was a terrible waste of money if she wasn't going to enjoy it properly. She no longer seemed able to think of the gems that she had produced in the past; the mock suicide attempt with the noose round her neck, tied to a ceiling bracket, her head jerked over to one side, her eyes wide open and staring . . . that time when she'd emptied the entire contents of their drinks cabinet down the sink, except for the drop of whisky which she'd rubbed into her skin so that she stank of the stuff, and they'd come back to find her, apparently comatose, on the bathroom floor. This was a pretty feeble effort by comparison. She didn't even bother to wait up to see her parents' reaction, but went into her room and hurled all the birthday presents into cupboards, except the locket, which she carefully removed, and the clock, which she placed on the bedside table.

When she was in bed she picked it up, turned it this way and that, and found that now, contrarily, she *wanted* it to work. She noticed a minute crack in the back of the clock, a hairline fracture of the wood. When she held it up to the light she could see that it formed three sides of a perfect rectangle, with the bottom of the clock forming the fourth side. This was very interesting. It looked as if it was meant to be opened. For a few minutes she toiled away with her fingernails, achieving nothing but the chipping of pearl nail varnish which she had worn, illegally, to school. Then she tried inserting a nail file, very carefully, into the crack, and to her delight the section swung open, like a little trapdoor. It seemed too much to hope that there might be something inside, but there was. Not the priceless jewel which had been Victoria's first idea, nor the little package of heroin that was her second, but a key, another little key like the one that wound the clock, only smaller. This must be the key to wind the alarm, then. No point setting the alarm when the clock wouldn't go, but it looked as if it badly needed winding, so she wound it anyway. It was really rather intriguing, a secret little space like that. Perhaps she would invest some of her savings and get the clock mended.

As she set it down again there came the sound of a key in the front door; hastily she switched her light off. Noises of fury — "Oh my God, Simon, it's like a bar-room in here" and her door was opened — "I don't believe for one moment that you're asleep, Victoria" — but she didn't stir, and they must have decided that it wasn't worth the hassle, because the door closed again, and soon the moans of "I'm fed up to the back teeth with her" . . . "What am *I* supposed to do about it" . . . faded into: "That idiot of a Martin! That lunatic! You won't believe me when I tell you the things he did! I had this fantastic hand, six spades to the ace queen jack . . ."

Victoria went to sleep.

THREE

The sound of the alarm was like a pneumatic drill boring into Victoria's brain. She shouted three words at it, all of them obscene in varying degrees, and tried, as usual, to go back to sleep. But there was a noise, an insistent repetitive noise that just shouldn't have been there; try though she might, she couldn't ignore it. Reluctantly she unburied herself, and hazily, through lingering layers of sleep, the truth clicked into place. Her clock was ticking.

But how could that be? And — wait — something else was wrong. An alarm had gone off. Well, then, it must have been the alarm on her new clock, for wasn't the old one kaput? Victoria sat up, trying to assemble these facts into some sort of logical order. It was impossible; it couldn't be explained. The alarm dial on the new clock was still pointing to around fifteen, midway between fourteen and fifteen, which meant it would go off at about half past two in the afternoon. What was the time now? She looked at her watch — just past a quarter to eight. Precisely the time that her old alarm had always been set for. And the ringing noise had been very familiar. It had sounded, in fact, exactly like . . .

Her old alarm clock was ticking too. This was too much. Victoria got out of bed, picked it up, shook it, examined it. It looked exactly as normal, but then it would, for there had been no external signs of yesterday's injury. It had just stopped, and now it was going like crazy. *Both* clocks. How could it happen?

At this point her mother looked in, registered surprise at seeing Victoria on her feet, nodded in acknowledgement, and left. She didn't mention the cigarettes. Either she wasn't yet conscious

24

enough to have remembered, or else they were saving it up for a good doodah at breakfast.

This, anyway, now seemed quite unimportant. As she dressed Victoria's mind was fully occupied with this business of the clocks. Their behaviour seemed senseless, ludicrous. But there must be an explanation — there always was an explanation for everything. Take the alarm clock first, the familiar object. Obviously it had started to work again during the night; therefore it must be possible for a clock to suffer an injury that was temporary only. But the alarm? She hadn't set it the night before. Ah, but when the clock had hit the wardrobe it had been cut off in mid-ring, hadn't it? So when it started working again, and came round to seven forty-five, it finished the ringing from the day before.

So much for that one. But the new clock? It, too, must have sprung into life during the night, while she slept. But how — why? Had the change in temperature somehow affected the mechanism of the clock, and caused its parts to start moving? She did keep her room very warm. It wasn't a satisfying answer, but there was no other. Victoria had always been very impatient with people who talked to plants, or claimed that machines simply wouldn't work for them, as if such things had hearing, feelings and powers of identification. Such people would probably say the clock had started because it was happier in its new environment, or something equally fatuous. But *both* clocks! Still, her deductions must be correct. There was no conceivable alternative.

And now, of course, she was late for breakfast, and would probably be late for school.

"It's stone cold by now," said her mother, "and you were up so early, as well. I don't know what you've been doing but I'd be surprised if it was worth the waste of a good breakfast." Victoria didn't bother to explain; food was more important than talk, and she rarely said much at the table. Still they said nothing about the cigarettes. It must be their new policy, to ignore her behaviour altogether, unless they were simply too much occupied with the post mortem on last night's bridge. The loathsome Martin had, this morning, been displaced as chief criminal by Sheila Everett, her father's bitterest enemy.

25

"I think that woman deliberately throws games away when she's playing with me. Grown men would weep to hear the things she did to me last night. I've told her before: if she's sick she should go to a doctor, not a bridge club. I shall never play with her again. If she cuts into my table, I shall cut out . . ."

Victoria had heard it all before. She could remember her father saying exactly the same thing, word for word. Briefly she considered pointing out that if he really wasn't going to play with this stupendously subnormal Sheila he should stick by what he said, and save himself, and everyone else, the misery. But she wasn't really interested enough to bother, and in any case her mother was anxious to get in and offload the burdens of partnering people whose ability to add up to thirteen must be seriously in doubt.

She really was late by the time the last forkful of cold bacon had joined the last piece of congealing egg in her stomach, and then she couldn't find her school shoes, the ones she'd had at Christmas. They couldn't be far, but there wasn't time to look. Fortunately her old ones hadn't been thrown out, and miraculously they still fitted, so she wore those. The yard was empty when she reached the school, so the first bell had gone, and probably the second bell too. She scurried indoors and up the stairs to her formroom — they were just going down for Assembly. She missed her usual place between Lesley and Sophie, and had to tag along with the tailenders.

Assembly was, in Victoria's view, a totally pointless exercise. The only useful bit was the notices and announcements at the end, but most of the time they had nothing to do with you anyway, and could equally well have been distributed as notes in the form registers. But no — every day they must all troop down to the hall and endure fifteen minutes, at the very least, of brain-boggling boredom. Today was typical. The ceremonial march of the head mistress, deputy head and a prefect on to the stage. The announcement and rendition of hymn number 391, omitting verses four and five. The lesson, sounding, as always when delivered by that cocky redheaded prefect, like an elocution exercise. Then prayers. Victoria did not see how any rational person could believe in God. To her mind he was roughly on a par with astrology, only marginally less interesting. It was amusing, flicking through a paper, to see what the stars had in store for you that day; God wasn't even enterprising enough to announce his intentions. Maybe a few thousand years ago, when they hadn't understood about science, they'd needed some sort of magic to explain things, so they called it God, or Allah or whatever. Our Father, which art in heaven! Her father was in his office in St. John's Wood, and heaven a fantasy for people afraid to face the reality of death, and then everlasting nothing. For ever and ever, amen.

Then the notices. The fifth year were holding yet another sale of home-made cakes in the hall at break, in aid of Social Services; the under-sixteen netball team were playing Radford school tomorrow, and so on and so forth. Finally, the triumphal exit of the headmistress, deputy head and prefect, followed by the dismissal of the proletariat, line by straggling line. And so to business. It's Friday, it's twenty-five past nine; it must be Maths.

Lesley had had a haircut. Yesterday's rampant locks were now trimmed and shaped into a tidy, thickly fringed cap. "When did you manage that, then?" Victoria asked in some bewilderment, as she got out her Maths stuff. "Did your mother do it?"

"What?"

"Your hair, klutz."

"What about my hair?"

"It's been *cut*."

Lesley looked at her oddly, and said: "You're calling *me* a klutz? I had my hair cut on Tuesday. You know I did. What's the matter with you — lost your memory or something?"

Victoria would have retorted very sharply indeed, but at that moment Mrs Durban came in, and she had to hold her tongue. Silently she seethed. Clocks, Lesley — everyone was potty. She was the only sane person in this whole crazy world.

Maths was one of the O Levels they were doing this summer, and Mrs Durban had been periodically entertaining them with gems from the old O Level exam papers, of which she had a seemingly endless supply. But today she caught herself out — Victoria soon recognized the problems she was writing on the board as ones she'd given them already. Nobody told her — why should they? A problem that has been grappled with before is an easier problem the second time round.

"Work quietly, please, in your rough books," said Mrs Durban, "and I'll be coming round to see how you're getting on." Victoria set to work, and finished all three in no time. She remembered where she'd gone wrong before, and then it was easy. Lesley was still slogging away at the first one, but then, Victoria had always been much better than Lesley at Maths and Science subjects. With languages it was the other way round; Victoria it was who wilted at the sight of a subjunctive. Well, she wasn't going to help Lesley, not when she was being so silly. Victoria sat back, and let her eyes wander.

She didn't like what she saw. It was odd — it was very odd indeed, and suddenly she began to feel uneasy. It was almost as if something *had* happened to her memory. Everybody looked different. Not dramatically so, but wherever she looked little things were wrong. She could count six — no, seven people who'd had their hair cut last night, and that was without including Lesley. Others had hair longer than she remembered. And two girls had acquired curls overnight, and three had lost them. Admittedly Victoria's class were constantly experimenting with their hair, and styles were changed all the time — but this was just incredible. And it seemed that nobody but herself had noticed. Then she caught sight of Philippa Barton, and now she did feel scared. For Philippa, who had always had the longest, glossiest hair in the class — it hadn't been cut since she was seven — had caused a great stir this term by appearing one day with the whole lot chopped off, and a wispy little pixie sort of cut in its place. There had been oohs and aahs and gnashings of teeth and wailings of "Oh, Phil, how could you?" Today, there was Phil with her old mane of hair glittering down her back like a golden waterfall.

It must be a wig. So what was wrong with that? Phil had regretted her decision, and bought a wig. But were wigs allowed in school? And why had nobody said anything? Nobody had nudged, pointed, shown the slightest surprise. Well — she had been late. Perhaps she'd missed all that. But Mrs Durban hadn't said anything either.

28

They must be playing a trick on her. It was a stunt, a belated birthday joke. Somehow they'd planned it the day before. They would all change their hairstyles overnight, and pretend that nothing had happened, and see how she reacted. It was conceivable . . . oh, no, it wasn't conceivable, because nothing could explain how Lesley had got herself such a professional-looking haircut after half past nine last night — and she hadn't been in a hurry to get rid of Victoria, or alarmed when she arrived, or giggling secretly — nothing. And — this was the crunch — they were not that sort of form. They had neither the unity nor the imagination to combine against her in this way, and in any case hardly any of them were the sort of people who would sacrifice a hairstyle for the sake of teasing Victoria Hadley. I'm not losing my memory, she thought, I'm losing my *mind*, something is very wrong — and then Mrs Durban arrived at her shoulder, and she had to pull herself together.

"Finished already!" she said, pleased but not unduly surprised at this performance from one of her best pupils. "Well, let's see — I'll leave the paper with you, and you can try number four while we're waiting for the others."

Victoria stared at problem four but could not make any sense of it. This one was new to her, and in her disturbed frame of mind there was no way she could tackle it. Mrs Durban, the only person in the room who looked really *right* — had anything ever changed about her in the four years she'd taught them? — went up to the board and started to work through the problems, but not one word that she said registered on Victoria's brain, until the bell went, and, picking up the blackboard duster, Mrs Durban said:

"You're all going to have to start getting down to some hard work. I know you're thinking that June is a long way away, but you'll be amazed at how quickly the time will pass — suddenly the exams will be upon you, and you'll have done nothing. This class is capable of some very good results, and that's what I'll be expecting of you in the Mock exam."

Victoria heard no more. Numbly she collected her books, stuffed them into her bag and wandered, almost unseeingly, out of the room. There was a conspiracy, a conspiracy to make her think that she was mad, and now Mrs Durban must be a part of it as well. For they had done the Mock O Level, had done it in January, and now it was March. It was March the eleventh, the day after her birthday. She knew this with one hundred per cent certainty; knew it as surely as she knew her own name.

Zombie-like she walked along the corridor and into the passage that ran along the side of the hall. There was a large cork notice-board here. Victoria stopped. The notices looked familiar enough — teams for forthcoming sports fixtures, a copy of the school rules, an artily stencilled poster advertising the school play, a notice about . . . NO! a voice screamed inside her head, for the school play had been performed in December. Well — someone had forgotten to take it down — or there was to be another, special performance . . . desperately she turned to the sports lists and read: St. Catherine's v Radford, 11 a.m. at St. Catherine's, Sat. October 9th.

"No, no, no," she said aloud, and then someone — Sophie — nudged her and said she didn't want to be late for Geography, did she? Victoria followed her blindly, neither knowing nor caring where she was going. There was a slight buzzing in her ears, and a terrible, lurching, nauseous feeling in her stomach, unlike anything she had ever experienced in her life. They turned in at a classroom door. Where — oh, Geography. She was in the Geography room. There was her desk, and she must get to it and sit down. She would feel better when she sat down.

"Victoria, are you all right?" This was Lesley. Her voice seemed louder than usual, her face swimmingly close. "Hey, *Vic.* You've gone white as a sheet." There began a buzz of voices — "she looks terrible" . . . "she's been very odd today" . . . but the insistent buzz inside her head was louder. She must sit down, and then it would go away.

"I'm fine," she said, and her own voice sounded distorted, magnified, it seemed to be coming out of her ears and floating over her head . . . but Miss Parr was waiting for order, and Miss Parr was the dragon of all dragons. She'd have made St. George run quivering home to his mother. Reluctantly they let Victoria be.

I mustn't be sick, she thought. But sitting down hadn't helped;

30

the buzzing was louder than ever now, and she *would* be sick if she didn't get out of the room, sick on the floor in front of everybody. She stood up and said something — she wasn't sure what, and now her voice was so faint that she could hardly hear it — about not feeling well, and could she go outside for a minute, please?

"Yes, of course," said Miss Parr, in such a kind voice that it sounded like someone else altogether, but nothing could surprise Victoria now. The last thing she saw in the room was the date, chalked on the blackboard: Friday, October 8th, 1982.

Victoria closed the door and leaned unsteadily against the wall outside. Rising to her feet had made her feel worse. I must go outside, she thought. I'll be better in the fresh air. *Please* don't let me be sick . . . She set off down the corridor. She couldn't feel her feet on the floor, but she must be walking, she was doing the right things with her legs and the walls were moving past her . . . But I really am ill, she thought, and then she felt, very distantly, and with no pain, the impact as she hit the floor. And then for a few moments she knew nothing.

When she came round she realized almost instantly, although it had never happened to her before, that she must have fainted. Even as she lay there, and in spite of all that had happened, some part of her mind was interested enough to file it away — so this is what fainting's like. Now I know. She had a dim memory of falling off her chair in the Geography room — and then, puzzled by the lack of attention, she moved her head, and saw where she was. Had she really asked permission, got up and left the room? She remembered thinking about it, but not actually doing it. She felt so very much better now. The nausea and the noise in her head had quite gone. Well, what a very strange thing. She had fainted. How annoying that there had been absolutely nobody to see it. She might never do it again.

"Vic! Oh, help! Look, she's passed out!" It was Lesley, who must have asked to go after her and see that she was all right, or perhaps old Parr had sent her — and then people arrived and took over, and soon she was lying on a bed in the sick bay, with a blanket over her and the blinds down. It was very comfortable, pleasant and relaxing; she closed her eyes, and soon drifted off into a peaceful sleep.

31

FOUR

By the time that Miss Wells, the younger and nicer of the two games teachers, came into the room, Victoria had been awake for some time. The events of the day had come back to her with a dismaying clarity, right up to her collapse in the corridor. What she wanted, desperately wanted, to believe was that all those odd happenings, the October Syndrome, as she grimly termed it, had been in some way hallucinations, distortions brought about by the build-up to the faint. But she feared that it might have been the other way around; that the fainting had not been the cause, but a direct result of the Syndrome. If only someone would tell her that it was March, of course it was March, she would never ever ask for anything more.

"How are you feeling now? You must have given yourself quite a bang when you fell."

Victoria sat up, wincing somewhat. "My elbow's sore, and the side of my head here, but only when I move or touch them. What's really bothering me is that I feel a bit confused. I can't remember properly what day it is."

"Friday," said Miss Wells, predictably.

"Yes" — how to put this without making them think she'd got amnesia or something, and have to go to hospital to be checked out? "Friday, that's right, and what's the date again?"

Miss Wells, who had a reputation for a pleasant kind of vagueness, most unusual for games staff who were generally very much on the ball, had to think about this one. "Well. Let's see — tomorrow we play Radford, that's October the ninth, so it's the eighth today." She looked at Victoria with some concern. "You seem to have concussion. I wonder if you should see a doctor."

"Oh no, I'll be fine," Victoria said hastily, for that was the last thing she wanted. If she even attempted to explain she'd probably be certified. Whatever this nightmare was that was happening to her, there could be absolutely no possibility of telling anybody. She was on her own.

"You really don't look very well," Miss Wells was saying. "I don't think there's much point in your rejoining your class now. You've missed most of the day anyway. How do you feel about it? Would you like to go home?"

"*Yes*," said Victoria. Impossible to contemplate getting through an afternoon with her class, when they were back in October, and she had lived through Christmas, the New Year, the January exams. She was in control of herself now, but it was the most fragile control, and under the slightest strain it would snap.

"Will anyone be in? Your mother? I'll ask the office to ring her."

"There's no need . . ." began Victoria, who hated her mother, with her lank, unwashed-looking hair and starkly unmade-up face, to come to the school under any circumstances. But Miss Wells ignored her, and a few minutes later Mrs Hadley arrived, looking surprised, as well she might, for Victoria was and always had been healthy to the point of absurdity. Childish ailments had scarcely touched her; bugs and viruses had apparently been rendered helpless by her tiny blonde person. She hadn't missed a day of school since the second year. "This isn't like Victoria," Mrs Hadley said, as if in apology, to Miss Wells. "It's not like you," she said to Victoria, reinforcing the point, as they walked home. A nuance of suspicion was detectable in her tone. Normally Victoria would have said something acid to the effect that she'd far rather be at school than at home, so why should she fake anything? — but she was much too subdued for that, and it seemed that her mother sensed it, for she said, more kindly: "What exactly happened, then?" and Victoria gave her the edited highlights, the part that could be told.

When they got home she found — and again this was unlike her — that she didn't want to retreat to her room, to be alone. "I think I'll just lie down on the sofa for a while," she said, wanting company for some reason; not demanding, testing company, just someone dull and familiar, someone who'd leave her pretty much to herself, but yet *be* there. For once, her mother was the ideal companion.

"Would you like the television on? I always have it on in the afternoons. There's usually something watchable . . ."

"No," said Victoria, as her mother advanced, button-pressing finger outstretched at the ready. No television — no radio, either, with its half-hourly news bulletins. She didn't want to hear October's news — stories to which she knew the ending, headlines that were history. It would be too disturbing.

"What about something to eat, then?" Mrs Hadley looked disappointed.

So that's what you do all day, watch the box, thought Victoria, no wonder you're miserable if that's your life, no wonder you're bored, no wonder you're boring.

"I could do you a ham and cheese omelette, you used to like that."

And instead of saying: "I feel bad enough without indigestion as well," or "what you do to ham makes me wish we were Jewish" — the like of which were her accustomed replies — Victoria said: "Yes please. I'd like that."

When her mother was safely in the kitchen, banging about in search of the omelette pan, Victoria did something else that she had never previously even considered. She went into her parents' bedroom and took one of the tranquillizers from the bottle on her mother's table. Or, rather, since her mother had been on the things for years, and had moved on to strong ones, she took a half, and threw the other half away. It was a calculated decision. She could feel the stirrings of panic rising within her again, and could think of no other way to combat it. She must try to remain in control. Control, or the fear of losing it, lay behind Victoria's normal instinctive dislike and mistrust of drugs and alcohol. She couldn't understand what made people want to mess around with them. But today was different. The usual rules simply didn't exist.

And it worked. She ate the omelette, and even as she was

34

finishing it off and stretching herself out again on the sofa, a rather pleasant doziness began to come over her. She found herself able to survey her predicament quite calmly; worse things had happened to millions of people and they'd kept their nerve. Maybe time did have its little accidents now and again; it was wrong to close your mind to any possibility, however unlikely it might seem. Who, a thousand years ago, would have believed in electricity, in atomic structure, in chromosomes and genes?

But if these little hiccups of time were commonplace, why was it that nobody knew of them? Quite impossible to believe that she, Victoria Hadley, out of this entire teeming planet, was the first to experience them. Perhaps, then, these lapses into the past were only brief, and when returned to normal time the subject was left with no memory of the experience, none at all. In which case countless people had gone through this; they were all walking around today with no knowledge of it whatsoever.

But what of the other people, the people around them? What, for instance, would happen if she were to predict to her mother, now, some event from the missing five months — would her mother remember the prediction when the event actually came round? She would try it and see. It must be something big enough to be memorable. Victoria racked her brains for some world headline from the relevant period, but her mind remained blank. All the big news from the spring and summer, the Falklands war, and World Cup, had been long over. What then? Ah — President Brezhnev had died, hadn't he? The Big Chief Red with the one thick eyebrow going right across his face. She was sure that had been quite near to the end of last year. Not that there was anything so stunningly brilliant about predicting the death of such an aged person. He'd been looking ready to conk out for ages. But she could think of nothing better.

"President Brezhnev," she said aloud. "I think he's going to die. I think he's going to die very soon."

Mrs Hadley had been flicking through a pile of magazines in a desultory sort of way, letting them slide to the floor when she'd finished with them. They would probably still be on the floor in a week's time. "Yes, I wouldn't be surprised," she said, without looking up.

"I'd bet everything I own that he will," said Victoria, wondering how to make an impression. "I'm convinced of it."

"Would you?" said Mrs Hadley, a little bewildered by this sudden onslaught. "I thought he'd been dead for ages," she said vaguely, "but perhaps I was thinking about someone else."

Which took care of that. Victoria hadn't quite realized the extent of her mother's indifference to, and ignorance of, world affairs. Was there nothing that would do? And then, to her alarm, she thought of a recent news story: the brutal murder of a little girl in North Wales. At this moment, that child and her family were going about their lives quite unaware of the horror that lay in wait for them. If the way it turned out was that she must live through every day until next March twice, then the life of that little girl was in her hands. She would be solely responsible for warning her parents, for saving her in some way. Oh, this was all so much more complex than she had realized. Why her? Why Victoria Hadley?

Her mother's voice startled her. "I'll make some coffee, shall I?" She had put the magazines down now, and for the last few minutes had been gazing aimlessly out of the window. She was such a depressing person. She seemed to have only two ways of addressing Victoria: either some kind of nag or complaint, or something to do with food. Often the two were combined, as in "You asked especially for sausages, so why leave them to go cold?" or "What's wrong with the custard *now*?"

"Yes, coffee," murmured Victoria. She dragged her mind back from the murder — she must think of the present, if you could call it that. For the moment, this one day was enough to handle. There was still the evening. It was Friday — had she arranged anything, perhaps with Daniel? How could she tell? Impossible to remember one individual day from five months ago. If only she kept diaries — but Victoria had never yet succeeded in keeping a diary past January the twelfth. And even if she had one, the entry for October the eighth wouldn't be there, would it, because she wouldn't have written it yet. Her mother, though — her mother would know. Mrs Hadley, however dubious her knowledge of the continued existence of world leaders, was generally well-informed on goings-on under her own roof, particularly on Friday evenings. For if Victoria was going out, she might well pop along to the club for a few hours, although it wasn't one of her regular nights. Yes, she would know. So when her mother came back with two mugs of coffee and some fruit cake, Victoria said:

"Perhaps, you know, I did have some slight concussion. I can't remember for sure what I was going to do tonight."

"Yes, I was meaning to say, do you think you'll be well enough to go? If so, I might go to the club for an hour or two."

"Go where?" said Victoria, with patience, "Where was I going?"

"To the pictures with Daniel, I thought you said. I'm sure you did say that."

Which was just what Victoria had feared all along. It was out of the question; she couldn't go. For Daniel was the one person she had no chance of fooling. She would be bound to make a slip; talk about something that hadn't yet happened, or, more likely, be unable to continue some conversation started a few days before — her memory would be very vague of what, to Daniel, would be the immediate past. Somehow she would give herself away, and then Daniel would pounce. There'd be no fobbing *him* off with vague explanations. He'd go on and on at her until he was satisfied with her answer. And she would have no answer. This was one thing, the first thing ever, that she couldn't tell him. He was too precious to be risked in any way.

"No, I don't feel like going out tonight," she said. "I'll ring him in a while and let him know." Although actually it was already half past four — she might as well do it now. Her mother was looking concerned, as if thinking that to give up an evening with Daniel Victoria really must be feeling rotten. Victoria interpreted her expression as disappointment at the prospect of an evening with no bridge.

"I was just going to ring you," said Daniel. "Sophie told me you'd been ill. How d'you feel now?"

"Lousy," said Victoria. "I don't think I can make it tonight. My head still hurts where I fell, and really I just want to rest."

"I'll come round instead, then, shall I?"

Oh dear, thought Victoria, for Daniel was so easily offended, so mortally wounded by the mere suggestion of a rejection, so eager to believe the worst. But to have him here, without even the distraction of the film to inhibit conversation, would be even worse than the cinema.

"No, I wouldn't, Daniel, because really I just want to go to bed and sleep. I don't feel up to talking, even."

"You only fainted, I thought," Daniel said, rather distantly. "But I suppose if you don't want to see me, you don't."

Victoria sighed inwardly. This was so hard, when half of her, the instinctive half, so badly wanted him to come over. But the rational half prevailed.

"Come tomorrow!" she said desperately; she would cope with tomorrow when it arrived. "I'm sure I'll be better then, after a good night's sleep. You can't imagine how peculiar it makes you feel, fainting. It's really horrible. Please come tomorrow, Daniel."

"Yes — all right," said Daniel, not sounding in the least appeased. "Morning or afternoon?"

"Whichever you like," said Victoria, and then, as Daniel was showing no signs of expressing a preference — "Make it the afternoon, then; you know how bad I am at getting up at weekends. Say two o'clock."

"Two o'clock, then," Daniel said, and with a muttered "Bye" he hung up. Victoria would have laid enormous odds that he'd ring back later, on some flimsy pretext, just to check that she really was there, unwell, and not sneaking off out with someone else. She found it enormously flattering that anyone should care about her so much; it was good to be cherished. But he did take it a bit far at times. It would also be good to be trusted.

Mr Hadley came back from his solicitor's office in St. John's Wood at ten to six, ate, changed, spoke a few words with his wife and daughter and departed for the bridge club precisely one hour later. It promised to be a very long evening for Victoria. Normally there would have been homework to be done — in a perverted sort of way Victoria quite enjoyed homework, as long as it wasn't French or English — but not today, although you could say that she had already done it. It occurred to her to look through one of her exercise books — her bag had been repacked and brought to the sick bay by Lesley. Out came her Biology book. Months of work had vanished, leaving clean, untouched pages. Or had they vanished? For this was the very same book as she had now, in March — but in an earlier stage of its existence. As far as it was concerned, all those diagrams and drawings and notes had never been there at all. They were in its future, so how could they be said to have *vanished*? God, but this was complicated. Without knowing quite what she had in mind, she wrote her name, Victoria Louise Hadley, just after the last piece of work in the book, a drawing of a locust, busily digging a pit for egg-laying purposes.

"Shall we have the television on now, then?" asked her mother, in tones of wearied patience. Victoria still couldn't face October's television, although on the face of it it would be no different from watching repeats. And in fact, on this day in October she had been out with Daniel all evening, so she wouldn't have seen the night's television anyway. But she said no just the same, out of bloody-mindedness. "I've got such a bad head still."

"Then you'd better go and lie down," her mother said, "because I'm not sitting here watching a blank screen all night." Victoria smiled sardonically as she got up. Her brief period of tyranny, granted because of illness, was clearly ended. And if she was to spend the evening in her room, and her mother gazing miserably at the box, then really her mother might just as well have gone to the club. But Victoria wasn't going to suggest it; let her suffer. Suffering was what she was good at, with all her complaints, her hard-done-by expressions and her tranquillizers. Victoria was starting to feel more like herself all the time.

She found the silence of the room, broken only by the ticking of the clock, strangely oppressive. She turned the heating up, and put a cassette on quietly. Then she curled up on the bed, plumping the pillows up against the wall behind her. There was a jumble of thoughts scrambling round inside her head. If only the Grand National had been run already! If she were to live again through all the lost time she would know the winner. She could put all her savings on it and make a pile of money. She had quite a respectable savings account, most of it put there by her grandmother. But then, she was too young to go into a betting shop, and no responsible adult would do it for her. Unfortunately Victoria knew no irresponsible adults, though there seemed to be plenty around, and perhaps she could find one . . . but this was all hypothetical. March the tenth was a few weeks too early for the National. Likewise the F.A. Cup Final, the World Snooker Championship — all the big things you could put money on, and whose winner she would have remembered. Just her rotten luck.

And what of the January exams? She knew all the questions, and after the exams they had gone through all the papers so thoroughly. She wouldn't be able to help getting phenomenally good results, which might be fun at the time, but where would it get her in the long run? She might be suspected of cheating. And even if she wasn't she could never repeat the results, and all the staff, their expectations raised, would give her a very hard time when she disappointed them in the summer. She would have to botch the exams deliberately, and that would not be easy, getting the balance right so that they were close to her normal performance. It seemed that there were no advantages whatsoever to be gained from all her advance knowledge — the reverse, if anything, she thought, remembering again the murdered child, and the near-impossibility that would be her task in trying to save it. For who would listen to a fourteen-year-old girl who claimed to have premonitions? To whom could she go anyway? She couldn't even provide the exact date or location. There were so many problems. And oh, the sheer monotony of living a second time through all those days without that element of surprise, of unpredictability, that takes the flatness from life and makes the bubbles sparkle. For nothing could happen that was not already known to her. Wherever she looked, the view was sombre.

Daniel rang back just after nine. "I couldn't remember what time it was you said to come," he said unconvincingly. "Was it two or three? Ah, right, two. I thought it was, but better to check. Listen — I'm sorry if I sounded a bit cross earlier. I was just — you know — disappointed — I didn't realize how bad you were. What have you been doing, then?"

"Oh dozing," Victoria said vaguely, wondering what he'd have done if her mother had said sorry, she can't come to the phone, she's asleep . . . Charged round to see for himself? He really was amazing, sometimes.

Her mother looked up from Hawaii Five O as she put the

phone down. "I forgot to give you this," she said, nodding at a letter which lay on the side table. "Second post. Sorry about that, it slipped my mind."

"Doesn't matter," said Victoria. It was one of her grandmother's fortnightly letters, and while she was always pleased to get them, this one she had read already. The locket, she thought, wandering back into her room — it's not here, Gran's still got it, perhaps she hasn't decided to give it to me yet. And all those other presents, still in their various shops. Her Christmas presents too — and suddenly she stood still in bewilderment. Just when she had more or less accepted that, like it or not, she was back in October, and everything around her, however odd, had at least been consistent in that respect, now here was something that sent it all haywire again.

The clock. It had no business whatsoever to be here in October. She'd never seen it until her birthday. And it had been here all day. How on earth had she failed to notice that this was wrong? It must have been that damned tranquillizer, making her dopey. Victoria began to feel nasty prickings running up and down her spine. Could all this be a trick after all, and the tricksters had overlooked the clock? But she knew it was impossible. Here was the postmark on her grandmother's letter: Oct 7. She tore the envelope open and skimmed through the familiar lines. There was no trickery. It was the clock . . . and then, with a conviction that amounted to certainty, she knew. This whole nightmare had been caused by that clock! It had to be. It all fitted now. The sheer impossibility of a clock that was stopped at twenty-five past nine not only starting up during the night, but telling exactly the right time in the morning! And that other little dial — the hidden key — it was all a wicked trap, it was nothing to do with alarms at all. The thing had no button, no lever for turning an alarm off — it didn't even look like an alarm clock. The little dial — and finally this clicked into place — pointing to midway between fourteen and fifteen — it didn't mean two thirty p.m. at all, it was nothing to do with that. *Fourteen and a half was the age she'd been last October.*

She recoiled in terror. It wasn't an alarm clock. It was a monster. She must get rid of it, get it out of her sight. But how?

41

Her instincts told her to hurl it out of the window, but so afraid was she now of the powers of the clock, powers that could not be comprehended or measured, that she dared not harm it. It might destroy her.

Finally, for she could no more have touched it than she could a heap of writhing insects, she picked the clock up in an old black jumper and hid it in the back of the wardrobe. At least she couldn't see it, hear that menacing ticking with all that it implied. But now she had worked herself up into a state again, and this time there would be no release. These last hours of the day were destined to be the most terrible. The effects of the tranquillizer had worn off, leaving her with what seemed, by contrast, to be heightened awareness, tension and fear. As the night drew on she sat hunched in her bed, shivering despite the warmth, her thoughts a maelstrom of panic and dread. The bad witches, malevolent goblins and lurking monsters that prowl through the nights and terrorize the darkness of childhood had never bothered Victoria. She hadn't believed in them. Now she was faced with something in which she must believe, yet couldn't understand, and it left her defenceless. She had no control over what was happening to her. And yet it was all her own doing! She, uninfluenced and unaided, had brought the clock home, had prised open the hidden compartment, turned the key — perhaps she had doomed herself to repeat these five months for ever and ever, for all eternity — every time she reached her fifteenth birthday she would be jerked back again — she would never know what it was to be sixteen, to grow up, to work, to have children, she would never see the world or meet anybody new, she would never even leave school — and yet she would go on and on living! And it might be even worse. Maybe now that she had been switched backwards once, she would go on moving backwards — wake up tomorrow to find herself only thirteen — be forced helplessly to watch her life slipping away in reverse, until one day she would find herself crouched in a membrane inside her mother's womb — and then, presumably, nothing.

FIVE

The birds had long been twittering outside, and the black of night
had faded into morning grey, when sheer exhaustion finally
overcame Victoria's body and mind, allowing her to sink into
fitful restless sleep. It seemed that only minutes passed before she
was awakened — awakened by her mother's voice, which was
saying a great many cross things, and there was a smell — a sour,
stale tobacco smell. Victoria reluctantly opened her eyes, and saw
a large blue ashtray containing ten cigarette butts.

"Way to behave . . ." her mother was saying . . . "stink of
tobacco . . . five years off your life . . . revolting habit . . . lung
cancer . . ." They were the most beautiful words Victoria had
ever heard. She raised her head, and Mrs Hadley's voice faltered,
for her daughter looked quite appalling. Her face was an ashen
grey; her eyes, surrounded by enormous dark circles, seemed to
have sunk into her head.

"Victoria! What's the matter with you? You see what happens
when you smoke! You look terrible. You look like death warmed
up. Are you ill?"

"I don't know," Victoria said. "I couldn't sleep. I had a very
bad night."

Mrs Hadley pondered. "Smoking," she said doubtfully, and
then: "Well, I don't know — you do seem poorly. Do you think
you should stay in bed today?"

Victoria looked around her. On her dressing table she could
see her grandmother's locket; next to it, her old alarm clock, quite
broken. Of the other, there was no sign. She was back in March.
Relief flooded her entire body like a tingling tide of warmth; to

43

her considerable dismay she felt her eyes prickling and burning, and huge wet tears began to run down her cheeks as she lay, silent and motionless.

Her mother stood there awkwardly, as if wanting to reach down and comfort her. But it had been so very long since she had seen Victoria cry, or display any weakness or vulnerability at all, that she no longer knew how. So she slipped out of the room for a while, her arrival in the kitchen bringing forth a diatribe from Mr Hadley about how that Martin Bailey was a criminal, an offence against society; his play of the cards was such butchery that the club ought to keep a meat cleaver for him on the premises; his bidding beyond rational belief. When Mrs Hadley went back Victoria had composed herself. Though piteously wan and haunted-looking, she was dry-eyed.

"Try to go back to sleep, Victoria," said her mother. "You can't go to school like that. You'd better take the day off."

"But isn't it Saturday?" asked Victoria in some confusion.

"No, Friday — yesterday was Thursday, your birthday, remember?"

Yes, she did, now. Her birthday — the cigarettes — she had arrived back at the day after that. Time had stood still while she'd been away. But it felt so very much like Saturday; she had just lived through one Friday, and now here was another.

"I'll leave you to rest, then," her mother said. Victoria slid out of bed and picked up the locket, fingering it hungrily, such a solid, tangible proof that everything was all right again. She was still holding it, her fist curled tightly, protectively, around it, when her mother looked in again a little while later, and found her sleeping like a baby.

When she woke again it was already afternoon, ten to two, and she felt incredibly, immeasurably better. Her mother, coming in with poached eggs and orange juice, was startled at the transformation. "I was going to get the doctor in if you still looked the same," she said. "It's so unlike you. I can't remember when you were last off school."

"No?" said Victoria, puncturing yolks with eager antici-pation. She was so hungry. Then she said carefully: "Have I never even had to come home in the middle of the day, then?"

"Not that I remember. I'm sure you haven't — unless I was out for some reason, and you didn't tell me. When did you mean?"

"I didn't mean anything," said Victoria. "Just thinking what a good record I've got." So the events of yesterday, her yesterday in October, hadn't happened at all. It was as if the day hadn't existed. She had been wondering about that, for on the surface she had changed the past, rewritten her own personal history, firstly by fainting and coming home, secondly by not going to the cinema in the evening . . . and she needn't have agonized over that at all, for it was clear that Daniel wouldn't remember. It was as if the normal one-way line of her life had sent out a little exploratory branch on October the eighth, creating two possible days and two possible futures leading from them. But the line had been abruptly cut off; it was a dead end. Everyone else who had been involved had forgotten it; they knew only of the main line version.

"Eat the eggs up," said her mother. "I'm glad to see some colour back in your cheeks. See what smoking does for you? No wonder you didn't eat that good stew I left for you last night. Best beef; none of that cheap stewing stuff. What time did you get back anyway? I rang you from the club while I was dummy once, about ten thirty, but it was engaged."

"Don't remember," said Victoria, pushing the emptied tray down the bed and fastening the locket round her neck.

"You've certainly taken to that locket." Another typical, lively mother-daughter conversation, thought Victoria — why does she say these things, doesn't she realize that there's no point to them, that they don't mean anything, that they aren't things that anyone would want to listen to? She was still on about the locket. "Your grandmother's had that for years; my father gave it to her when she was young. It's *very* generous of her to give it to you. What did you choose from Joe and Eileen's, then?"

"A pair of duelling pistols, with powder," said Victoria, and then, as her mother's lips went into the pre-tightening position — "Oh, all right. I got a pub mirror." Fortunate that she had been given the mirror as well, for she certainly wasn't going to mention the clock. She didn't even want to *think* about the clock. In a way

45

it was surprising that it wasn't there on the bedside table where she'd left it on the night of her birthday — the real yesterday — but then the thing seemed not to recognize or obey rules known to humankind. It might be in the wardrobe where she'd hidden it; it might not. Fervently she hoped that it had disappeared, had gone from her life for ever.

She got up then, wrapped her dressing-gown around her and went to examine her Biology book. It was completely up to date again, right up to the last set of notes from their double lesson on Wednesday afternoon. It seemed like eternities ago. She flicked back to the locust section; her name was gone, there wasn't the faintest imprint of it, just a smooth continuation of her notes, a description of the highly uncomfortable-looking procreative activities of the locust above. It was so weird — but she found some solace in the fact that there was a kind of wild logic to it. Nothing, absolutely nothing from yesterday, her October yesterday, had survived. It had all been cancelled, wiped out for ever like chalk cleaned off a blackboard. And this was without doubt the best possible thing.

Looking at her schoolbooks diverted her thoughts to the rest of IVA. They'd have had the regular Friday, Assembly, Maths, Geography — the one she'd been expecting at the start of that awful day. And wouldn't they be surprised that she hadn't turned up? She, Victoria Hadley of the iron constitution. Lesley would have been saying: "But she was round my place till nine thirty, and she was *fine* then . . ."

Lesley, in fact, appeared at the flat at quarter to four, her hair blessedly restored to the shaggy mess it should be. The concerned, visiting-the-sick expression that was ready on her face vanished as soon as she saw Victoria up and stomping round in her dressing-gown, looking much as normal.

"Florence Nightingale, I presume," said Victoria. "I'll have twelve crepe bandages, two dozen incontinence pads and a surgical truss."

"Skiving, eh?" said Lesley, perching on the arm of the sofa. "We all thought you had plague at the very least. Durban said that in Maths: if young Hadley's not here, then we must assume plague. She likes you, did you know?"

"So she should; I'm known to be a truly wonderful person," said Victoria. "Well, I like her, actually. Why not? She keeps her sadistic tendencies under control, which is more than you can say for most of them. No, but I really wasn't well, earlier. I felt so strange when I woke up. I thought for a while I was going to faint."

"The day you faint'll be the day I win Crufts," said Lesley, and Victoria smiled to herself — the final confirmation. "Anyway, I brought you the stuff from today to copy up, and I've written down what the homework is, all right?"

"So kind," said Victoria. "There's nothing so rallying as a French comprehension for an ailing person." There was, in fact, a French comprehension, but Lesley stayed for tea and they did it together, Victoria comprehending very little, and not caring in the least, so happy was she to have things back to normal, to be able to seal off that day and file it firmly away in a compartment marked "Discontinued".

In the evening Daniel rang again, taking advantage of his newly-discovered means of liberation, walking the dog. All this wasn't strictly necessary on a Friday, which was one of the nights he was allowed some degree of freedom, but Victoria guessed that he got some measure of enjoyment from this furtive thwarting of his father. She could never understand why he obeyed him at all, but presumably it made you a different person when you were brought up to that sort of thing; made you more docile and amenable to it. Victoria rarely saw Daniel on Friday nights now, anyway, for he preferred to get through as much as possible of the weekend workload at the first opportunity, leaving himself two days of relative relaxation. So he phoned her. They talked of this and that, and they even mentioned the other, but Victoria felt unaccountably depressed after he'd rung off. It was so long since she'd seen him — a whole extra day. At this rate she'd soon be forgetting what he looked like. Every time she saw her bayonet, these days, she thought of Daniel's father.

Later, when she was getting ready for bed, a bed, it seemed, she'd scarcely left, she finally summoned up the courage to look in the wardrobe. Unless she could convince herself that there was no danger, that she would wake up to Saturday, March the twelfth, there was another very bad night ahead. The clock was there, inside the jumper, just as she'd left it. It was silent — to all appearances, just another broken clock. And suddenly Victoria realized that as long as it stayed like that, as long as the hidden key remained unwound, then she would be safe. The key was the trigger; the clock had no way of harming her unless she interfered with it. But all the same, she didn't want to look at it. She'd work out what to do with it later.

The newly hung pub mirror definitely did something for the room. It reflected the bayonet perfectly, and you couldn't have too many bayonets, in Victoria's view. She slammed the wardrobe door shut and went to examine her reflection. She looked the same as ever — her experience had done nothing to her face, though she was sure she felt different inside. A bit special, certainly, but that was understandable, and it was more than that. Expanded . . . enlarged . . . as if something previously closed had been opened, somehow leaving herself, and the world around her, with more possibilities. Oh, it was impossible to describe. It was probably nonsense anyway. She went to bed.

SIX

Six full weeks passed before Victoria was able to bring herself to look at the clock again. Six weeks during which Easter came and went, and the summer term began; six weeks which saw Mrs Hadley become ever more depressed. She was prescribed a new variety of happy-pill, stronger than all its predecessors. Her bridge sessions became even more frequent than hitherto, weekdays and weekends alike, and twice Victoria heard her crying in the night. Mr Hadley said nothing about any of this; all that was heard from him was the steady irascible flow about the latest bridge atrocities that had been inflicted on his helpless person; about Sheila Everett, the bane of his very existence, the total palooka of all time; about people who would generally do much better to do the world a favour and take up tiddlywinks.

For Daniel Priestley they were six weeks of heavy, grindingly intense revision for his A Levels, Maths, Chemistry and Physics, which loomed like a black cloud. He turned up at Victoria's flat looking as pale and thin as an anaemic stick of celery, clad in a thin white T shirt and cotton trousers. It was by no means a warm day, but Daniel always appeared impervious to extremes of temperature. He wore heavy sweaters in August, while all around him were sweating and peeling off every garment that was decently possible; in mid-winter he appeared so skimpily dressed that it made your teeth chatter just to look at him.

"You look awful," Victoria said bluntly as she let him in. "You look like a plant that hasn't seen daylight for a fortnight."

"Yes, well, it's only for a couple more months now," said Daniel. "The staff keep telling us, these few months could be the most important of our lives."

"If you survive them. If you've still got the strength to write by the end of them."

"My mother keeps saying things like that," said Daniel, and Victoria sniffed; she had never been to the Priestley home, nobody ever did go there except Priestleys, but it was obvious to her that Daniel's mother's influence over what went on there was precisely nil.

"What you need is an hour's walk in the fresh air every day," she said.

"It wouldn't do any good," said Daniel. "I'd just see formulae and molecular structures everywhere, and electrons leaping out of the trees. It's all right. I can take it. My father wants me to get three A's."

"I thought Cambridge told you one A and two B's."

"Yes, but he thinks I can do better than that," said Daniel. "The trouble is, I'm not even sure that I want to go to Cambridge any more. It's so far away from you. Even if I came back down here every half-term, I still wouldn't see you for weeks on end. I could easily go to university here in London. That would be much better."

"I don't somehow see your father allowing you to turn Cambridge down," said Victoria, rather despondently; she herself had long been dreading what she saw as Daniel's inevitable departure for Cambridge in the autumn.

"We'll see about that," Daniel said mutinously, but this brave talk was easy now; it would be a different matter saying it to his father. "Where are your parents, anyway? Isn't your mother in?"

"Playing bridge," said Victoria. It was a Saturday afternoon, and both parents had departed at one thirty, in order to get a full five-hour session in.

"You mean you didn't tell them I was coming?"

"Yes, I did — why not?"

"And they've gone off and left us here alone? I don't believe it."

50

"Oh, come on, Daniel, they know you're too much of a gentleman to do more than give me a brotherly peck on the cheek." It had taken two months of acquaintance before he'd even managed that.

"But that's amazing. I mean — the thought of Dad going out and leaving Sophie alone in the house — with a boy! I just can't believe it."

"Daniel," said Victoria, with the usual mixture of amusement and irritation — it was almost as if he *wanted* a chaperone hovering in the shadows, guarding her virtue – "have you any intention of molesting me? Speak the truth, now."

"No!" he sounded most alarmed at the suggestion.

"Well, I've no intention of molesting you either, so relax, we're quite safe, neither of us is going to get pregnant. Now, shall we go into my room, or stay out here in case the sight of a bed might prove too overwhelming?"

"Don't say things like that, Victoria. I don't like you to talk like that."

"My room, then," said Victoria, for even in their absence the living-room was parent-territory, or mother-territory at least — her magazines everywhere, like a dentist's waiting room, her knick-knacks, her clutter, the general mess she always created around her, her mother-smell — she would be there, an invisible presence, a heavy depression moving in over southern England from the Continent. Ideally, Victoria thought, they should go out for a walk; that was what Daniel needed, but Victoria didn't get enormous kicks from walking. People who took exercise for the sake of it always struck her as slightly deranged. In any case, the sky was darkening with heavy cloud, and even as she spoke the first rain had begun to dash against the windows. So they made coffee and took it into the bedroom, Daniel still muttering about how unbelievable her parents were; he couldn't understand it at all.

"Of course you can't," said Victoria. "It's because neither of us had an average family. They're opposite extremes. Your parents — well, your father cares too much about you, and mine don't care about me at all."

Daniel hesitated at this criticism of his father, something he

51

wasn't used to hearing, but said: "Of course your parents care about you. That's a terrible thing to say."

"It's the plain truth," said Victoria. "Have you ever seen my father? As far as he's concerned I don't exist, except as an occasional drain on his income. And he doesn't seem to exist either. I'd hardly notice if he disappeared tomorrow."

"My mother's a bit like that in a way," said Daniel after a moment's thought. "I mean, she hardly exists either. She's always there, but she just seems to scuttle around in the kitchen, making food and serving it, washing and cleaning and that, that's all she does really, that's all she is."

"But that's dreadful! Doesn't she mind? Why doesn't she do something about it?"

"Well, you know, women get pleasure from that sort of thing, don't they, cooking and stuff. I don't know. She doesn't say anything."

"Oh, Daniel, surely you can't believe in this day and age that all a woman needs in her life is to cook the best roast dinner south of Watford and to choose the right washing powder to get that extra bluey-whiteness, and to keep her kitchen spotless with bloody Ajax to show her family how much she loves them — you can't believe that rubbish."

"I don't believe that, I didn't say that," said Daniel. "But . . ."

"She must be bored out of her brain. Has she got a brain?"

"Of course she has, she used to be a librarian before she got married, but . . ."

"Well then, why doesn't she go back to it? You and Sophie are practically grown up, why doesn't she go back to work?"

"My father wouldn't let her," said Daniel, surprised, as if this should have been obvious. "He wouldn't dream of it, his wife working. He thinks, you know, a man goes out and earns the money and a woman stays at home. I know it sounds a bit old-fashioned, but . . ."

"You bet it does! Old-fashioned! He's decided that she's got no option but to be an unpaid domestic servant for the rest of her life!"

"Well, it's not quite like that," said Daniel uncomfortably — "she's got a nice home, hasn't she, much better than she could

52

ever have afforded on her own, and a holiday abroad every year . . . all sorts of good things . . . and my father, well, he's just a person with very strong ideas, that's all. He won't let my mother wear any bright colours, reds or pinks or oranges or anything, all her clothes are sort of drab browns and greys. He thinks that women only wear brightly coloured clothes when they're trying — you know, to attract other men, sort of thing. My Auntie Sylvia gave her a red dress once, she'd been given it and it didn't suit her, so she gave it to my mother — and when my father saw it he cut it up, he got these scissors and cut it to shreds, and he called her . . . he called her things, you wouldn't believe what things. I was only about ten, I had to look it up in a dictionary, and even then I didn't understand."

"But, Daniel, why does she put up with it?" asked Victoria, when this had sunk in. It sounded like something from a bad film. "Nobody should live like that. I think she should leave him. I think she should have left him years ago."

"Leave my father? You don't understand, Victoria. He's a good man, he cares about us, you know, and you don't just leave like that, not when you've married someone, you don't break up a family. He's always been a good husband to her. He works hard, he works overtime, he gives her plenty of housekeeping money — he'd always provide for us. He'd die rather than let any harm come to us. You don't just break up a marriage because it isn't perfect. Nothing's perfect."

There were many things Victoria could have said to all this, but where was the point? Daniel was the product of his background, and presumably blinkered to the fact that the greatest service Mr Priestley could do for his children would be to throw open the doors and let them breathe. Of course, these things were always clearer to an outsider. When Daniel left home and got away he would probably see things in better perspective. But — oh dear — if he really did stay in London no doubt he would continue to live at home. He'd be at home until he was twenty-one or more. In a way, if you took the long view, it would be better if he went to Cambridge. At least he'd be away from his father's influence. He wouldn't like it, would he, the old rat, his kids escaping from his claustrophobic clutches? Maybe he did

53

want Daniel to go to Cambridge, but he thought of Cambridge, no doubt, as a sort of boarding school. He'd do everything in his power, short of walling them in, to keep his children in his stinking rancid nest. Well, they'd see about that. It wasn't going to happen to Daniel; she wouldn't let it. Sophie would have to look out for herself. Victoria rather thought she would be all right — she had detected dark seeds of rebellion lying deep within Sophie. When their season came they would burst out, and Sophie with them. For Mrs Priestley there seemed no hope at all.

"I could understand your mother being miserable," Victoria said, "although you say she isn't. But here's my mother, free as a bird, the whole world open to her, and she's miserable as sin." She told Daniel about the crying and the tranquillizers, and the way her mother mooched around all day at home, with only the television for company. "It's so stupid. I don't know why she doesn't work — *my* father wouldn't mind, he wouldn't give a damn, be glad of the extra money probably. She used to work, you know, up until about six years ago, she had a good job with a Building Society. Then one day she just stopped."

"It's the wrong way round," Daniel said. "You'd think she'd stay at home while you were little and then go back to work when you were older."

"Yes, it's potty. God knows what she's gained by it. I thought at least that being at home she'd keep the flat a bit cleaner, we wouldn't live in a pigsty any more, and perhaps even her cooking might improve, but everything's still the same old mess. And she's so boring, Daniel — she never says anything interesting, or does anything, she just sits around here till the evening and then she goes to play bridge. That's all she does."

Daniel frowned his disapproval of what sounded to him like extreme parental neglect. "Why can't she play bridge in the afternoons, then, and stay in in the evenings? She's really got it all wrong. She worked when you were little — that's all wrong. A mother should be with her child. No wonder you've got such a bad relationship now."

"She never goes to the bridge club without my father," said Victoria. "Never. And she's not interested in spending time with me. That's not the point. The point is, she should work during the day. It'd do her good. She wouldn't look such a mess all the time, then; she'd have to make an effort. I hate the way she looks. And she wouldn't have so much time to be miserable. Oh, for God's sake, Daniel, haven't we got anything better to talk about than parents?"

"Yes, but your mother . . ." said Daniel, and it was then that Victoria, who had quite enough of her mother as it was, and who had only brought the subject up in order to complain about what a boring flop of a person she was, decided to create a diversion by bringing out the clock. She had been toying with the idea all day, for the passage of time had not only dulled her fears, but had enabled a great deal of curiosity to build up inside her. Curiosity that held her back from throwing the clock away, that made her want more and more to get to grips with its baffling secret — to find out what made it tick. She was quite sure that it was harmless unless the little key was wound. For the first few days after her time-lapse she had thought, not unnaturally, of little else; even as the days stretched into weeks it remained uppermost in her mind. Several times now she had opened the wardrobe and gazed at the black jumper with what almost amounted to longing. But something, some lingering wariness, held her back. Now, though, with Daniel here, everything felt so safe. Daniel the scientist, she thought, as if the very fact of his A Level knowledge would dazzle the clock into normality. Now was the moment.

"What's that then," said Daniel — "a clock? What were you hiding it in there for? Let's have a look. Doesn't it go?" He turned it this way and that. "I'm not much good with clocks."

"I didn't expect you to fix it. I just wondered what you thought of it." It did sound daft. A clock was a clock was a clock. But, much to her gratification, Daniel seemed interested.

"I wish I could mend clocks, make them go. What's this here, this one to twenty-four dial?"

"What d'you think? I'm not sure." It would be so much easier to tell him now than it would have been on the day — the story would, surely, be more convincing told in retrospect. But not convincing enough, she decided sadly; he wouldn't believe it, and she couldn't expect him to.

"If it went up to thirty-one I might think it was some kind of

55

calendar. But twenty-four — what comes in twenty-fours except hours in a day? And yet the big dial only goes up to twelve, like an ordinary clock . . . I wish I could work it out. It really looks as if it's there for a purpose, doesn't it? Where did you get it?"

"My uncle's junk shop. He didn't know anything about it. He was going to throw it away." Victoria had phoned her uncle with some cautious questions about the origins of the clock, but he'd had no idea where it had come from. He'd thought someone must have brought it in while Eileen was in the shop, and Eileen had thought *he'd* got it from somewhere, and in the end they'd decided it must been something to do with that girl they'd had helping on Saturdays for a few months. Odd, wasn't it? It had just sort of appeared, one day . . .

"Mmm," said Daniel, and then, hopefully: "I'm sure I could think much more clearly if I had something to eat." When he said this his entire expression changed to what Victoria called his starved spaniel look; it was as if a sign saying: 'Feed Me' had appeared around his neck. Victoria liked feeding Daniel, which was somewhat alarming, in view of the conversation they'd just had. Was there some mechanism built into all females that caused them to derive pleasure from giving food to people they were fond of? She certainly wouldn't have believed it of herself until Daniel came on the scene, and here she was, making toast and jam for him, and positively enjoying it. She must have been conditioned without realizing it. Very unhealthy.

Daniel had lost interest in the clock when she returned with toast, biscuits and more coffee. This was disappointing; secretly she had hoped that he would instantly recognize its unusual properties, would say: "But Victoria, don't you realize what this is? You must have travelled back in time" — bringing it out into the open for her. She did so badly want to tell him. But he had put it down and was pottering about by the dressing table, looking in her letter-rack.

"Cheek!" said Victoria, setting the tray down.

"Who do you know in Hambourne?" asked Daniel, sounding somewhat disturbed. "There's dozens of letters here, all postmarked Hambourne. Who are they from?"

"Oh rats, you've discovered it, my secret lover," said Victoria, and then, as Daniel was looking distinctly unamused: "My grandmother, you king amongst twerps." It must have killed him, not to open one of them and examine the signature — or perhaps he hadn't had time.

"Oh, I see . . . yes, your mother's mother, she lives in Kent, she gave you that locket."

"That's the one," said Victoria. A suitable photo of Daniel had been acquired by means of trial and error, Victoria snapping away with her Polaroid until they managed to produce a picture with Daniel's head the right size. It was a bit fuzzy, but good enough.

"You know what I was thinking," Daniel said — "I know it sounds stupid, but that boy-friend you had before, that Keith, I thought for a moment he'd moved to Hambourne, and that was the reason you'd stopped seeing him, and all this time you'd been writing to him behind my back. I did think that, for a moment."

"Did you ever meet Keith Bellamy? No. Well, I promise you, nobody who'd seen you even *once* would want to go near him again. He was a human zero."

"You must have had some reason for going out with him," grumbled Daniel, and Victoria explained for the millionth time, it was just for convenience, she could see now that it had been a mistake but she hadn't known that then, and as for Daniel, she hadn't even met him, had she? It was all past, and what did it matter now?

"I suppose not," said Daniel; his face lightened a little, and he began to eat. Victoria sighed. Building up Daniel's ego was going to be a long, hard job.

But food is a great unwinder; soon Daniel had relaxed again, and began to talk about his revision. This led to a conversation about the education system, and the examination system, and the glaring flaws in both, and soon they had between them created an educational Utopia, a system of practicality and flexibility, a syllabus of topicality and relevance, a framework which catered for dunce and genius alike, which would make learning such fun that school holidays would become times of general mourning for children of all ages. These discussions of theirs, which had covered topics from racial tension to space

57

exploration, from cloning to baby-battering, had developed into a major pleasure for both of them. Victoria could, and did, talk to Lesley for hours on end, but their relationship centred around flippancy; any attempt to discuss race would soon dissolve into hysterical laughter as Lesley related one of her brothers' jokes about this Chinaman, Irishman and West Indian who went into a chemist's shop. A discussion on baby-battering, with Lesley, would become a macabre black comedy as they debated what weapons they personally would select for the wholesale destruction of their own offspring. As for Daniel, expressing his own opinions was something quite new for him. At first he hadn't seemed to realize that he had any. Victoria had been forced to say, over and over: "I don't care what your father says, I want to know what *you* think, Daniel, I really want to know." Now, he relished their conversations even more than she did.

Victoria sometimes wondered if they weren't a bit odd. This wasn't what you were meant to do with your boy-friend — sit and talk. You were supposed to smooch in the back row of the cinema — they'd given up the cinema before Christmas, when they'd both discovered that they were only going because they thought the other enjoyed it. You were supposed to doll yourself up and go to discos — Daniel, at a disco! The boy-friend was meant to make strenuous efforts to insinuate his hands under your clothing, efforts which you allowed to go so far and no further — every girl knew exactly where 'so far' was — and then reported with glee to your friends the next day. That's what Keith Bellamy had done, the one time she had been unwise enough to allow him back to the flat while her parents were out. He had sneaked his arm around her, started to dribble into her ear in his uniquely nauseating way, and had said, had actually said: "Don't you think you've got too many clothes on?" Victoria had been obliged to say sharply: "Will you keep still? I'm trying to count your blackheads." She and Daniel were so much better — they'd got it right, she was sure. They'd got *some*thing right.

The afternoon began to be evening, and when Mrs Hadley phoned at seven Victoria told her no, stay where you are, play the evening session as well if you want. It was only when Daniel was leaving at half past ten — his father locked the doors at eleven —

that he said, casually: "Did you know, by the way, there's a little bit in the back of your clock that opens up, and there's a key inside. I thought it might be the answer, but when I wound it nothing happened at all. Oh well. Never mind."

Why not? Why not, thought Victoria, her heart throbbing with excitement, anticipation and nervousness — the damage was done, the clock was set. And now at last she admitted to herself that for at least three weeks she had known that she must try the clock again. Didn't she want to be a scientist? How could a scientist miss such an opportunity? Her fear and panic now seemed remote and ridiculous — really, she'd behaved very badly, and it was a good thing that nobody would ever know. It would be different this time, for she knew the set-up: that nothing she said or did in whatever past she was taken to would matter, she was quite safe from repercussions — so she could do whatever she liked, which would be fantastic in itself — and after one day she would return to the present. Well, the decision was out of her hands now. The little hand on the dial had been moved during Daniel's fiddlings — it was now pointing between eight and nine, closer to eight. So be it. Eight years old. What had she been like? What had been going on in her life? Soon she would know.

SEVEN

All the furniture was in the wrong place. So was the window, and the door had disappeared altogether. Victoria blinked with all the confusion of one who wakes up in a place where she has no recollection of going to sleep. Ah, there was a door, there on the left in the corner. And then the strange shapes took on a lurchingly nostalgic familiarity, and she knew the room. She was back in her bedroom in their house, the only house they'd ever owned, 24 Fairfax Road. Her biggest and best bedroom ever, with its windowsill broad enough to lie on, its built-in cupboard, a cupboard like a little room, with a light inside. You could walk in and shut the door; shut the world out.

And there, on the table beside her, was the clock, ticking away brightly. Nearly a quarter past seven — had she really woken so early? It seemed so. The sky outside was light, but all was quiet. The frenzied zoom of traffic hadn't yet got under way; London was still waking up.

It was staggering. On the face of it, it was no more remarkable to be taken back seven years than it was five months — both were equally unlikely. But the first time there hadn't been a change of *place* involved. This time she had been physically moved, into a different room, a different *bed*, and she had slept through the whole thing. She looked at the clock with some awe, and realized immediately that the very first thing she must do was to hide it. Her mother would be coming in to wake her, and there was absolutely no way that a child of eight could have acquired a clock overnight. It could not be explained, so it must be

60

concealed. The cupboard. She wriggled out of bed, and, as her feet touched down, froze in astonishment — had the bed really been so high? Her *legs* — they were so thin, and her arms too — her hands so tiny — but of course, she was only eight! She was a fifteen-year-old brain in an eight-year-old body. The last time, the physical regression had been too insignificant to notice. But now! The clock forgotten, she rushed to the mirror — the furniture all seemed so high! — and there she was, her eight-year-old self.

With total absorption, Victoria surveyed her small form — the flat chest, the narrow hips, the almost genderless shape of a child. Her hair was so blonde, so baby-fine — had it really darkened so much as she'd grown older? Her round face, with its big blue eyes, its little turned-up nose, its perfect pink and white skin, as yet untouched by the greasy perils of adolescence. Victoria had only had a very few spots, but they had been a few too many. Like a tiny angel, she thought, in admiration. It was almost a shame that she'd had to grow up. Not that she'd really want to be without her teenage curves, such as they were, which wasn't much, unfortunately — but oh, hadn't she been sweet? There was no photograph that really captured it, for Victoria had always derived great satisfaction from thwarting would-be photographers with hideous grimaces and rolling of eyes. Perhaps that hadn't been so clever after all.

There was a muffled, high-pitched ringing sound, which had to be her parents' alarm going off. Speedily she hid the clock away — it should be used to cupboards by now — and bounded back to bed, revelling in the unaccustomed lightness of her body. Such a minute little waif she'd been. She must have shot up incredibly quickly at some point.

"Oh, you're awake," said her mother, coming in and then disappearing almost immediately, before Victoria had seen her. She seemed to be in a hurry — perhaps she was still working, then. There'd been none of this slouching around in dressing-gowns in those days. When exactly had she given up work? It had been during that long, searingly hot summer, the year of the drought and the ban on hosepipes and the crazy rain-makers. But what year had that been? She couldn't remember. Where were

61

they now? The dial had been set at roughly eight and a quarter, so it was 1976, summer 1976. June or July, probably. It must be a weekday, or they wouldn't all be getting up early, and it couldn't be much later than July the twentieth, or school would have broken and she wouldn't have been called.

There were some clothes, not very neatly folded, on the chair by the window; presumably these were what she was to wear. Also the front door key, which she wore round her neck on a chain. She had absolutely refused to wear it on an ugly piece of string. There was a thin dress, yellow and orange flowers, very summery — she'd always quite liked that dress, but had never admitted to this because her mother had chosen it. White knickers, and a white cotton vest. Vests! She'd certainly never imagined she'd wear one of those again. She had another good look at her reflection in the underwear, and heaved a sigh of regret for something lost that could never be retrieved. If she really could go back to being eight, she could train to be a ballerina, perhaps, or a gymnast, or an ice skater — all those possibilities had been open to her then, but at fifteen it was too late. All those doors were closed; the time had gone. Eight was the age she'd been when a young Rumanian gymnast called Nadia Comaneci had stunned the world with her Olympic performances, and Victoria, mesmerized, had joined the rush to enrol at a nearby children's gymnastics class — but soon after that they had sold the house and moved away, and in the general turmoil gymnastics had been forgotten. Oh — if only.

She pulled the dress over her head and went out on to the landing, where she found she had to think for a second before turning the right way for the bathroom. It felt so strange to go downstairs for breakfast — quite an expedition, after the flats, where all the rooms were on top of each other. Why, oh why had they ever given up this house for that poky little dump in Ladbroke Grove? At the time, though she had complained bitterly, she had accepted it, the way children do accept things, but it seemed very odd now. It must have been to do with money. And yet, how could it have been? It wasn't as if her father had lost his job. He'd been earning more and more all the time as his clientele increased and his reputation spread. She knew he was doing well, earning good money. So why? She'd have to think about it.

She padded down the mustard-coloured stair carpet. There was the old hall — the front door with its six little panes of opaque glass, the rag rug in front of it — and there was her mother in the kitchen, fully dressed already, pouring cornflakes into a bowl. Victoria stopped, and hung back almost with shyness, for this woman with her frothy fair curls, her round face with its frosty pale pink lipstick, her crisp, clean-looking white scoop-neck blouse and flowered skirt — this very model of a well-turned out young woman was so very far removed from any mother that Victoria knew or remembered. Had she really looked like this? She looked fifteen years younger, not seven.

"Take your cereal, will you? We haven't got all day." The voice was much the same, at any rate. Obediently Victoria picked up the bowl and took it through to the dining room. This wasn't an eating-in kitchen. There had seldom been bacon, sausages or kippers in 1976 — just toast if you were lucky, and cereal. No table laid — it was practically self service. Her mother hadn't had the time. There was her father now, rattling around in the bread bin. Mr Hadley had never been a cornflake person. He always eyed cornflakes as if he found them despicably common.

"Don't forget you've got swimming today," said Mrs Hadley, bustling in with a mug of coffee. She switched on Radio One. "I've put your things out by your satchel." Victoria glanced across the room at the monstrosity that was the satchel: pale brown plastic with dark brown straps and buckles. About as unchic as anything she could imagine. Beside it lay a mauve bag which she vaguely remembered making bits of in sewing; the teacher had done most of it, including the flower on the front, Victoria losing patience after the first petal. All this old garbage that had been thrown out years ago — all resurrected. Creepy. But she wasn't afraid — not one bit, for this time she had known what to expect, and she felt in control of the whole thing. It was all immensely interesting. Even her parents were interesting.

In came her father. *He* hadn't changed — his hair was a bit thicker, perhaps, and it hadn't yet started to recede at the temples, but the heavy black eyebrows, the thick-rimmed glasses,

63

the thin mouth that always seemed to be verging on a sneer — they were all just the same. He had never really looked young. He nodded politely at Victoria as she sat down, as if he knew her but couldn't remember from where, and was reluctant to start a conversation in case he gave himself away.

"It's going to be another scorcher," said Mrs Hadley, and the DJ on the radio promptly confirmed this. This is the right way to have breakfast, thought Victoria — who cares if it isn't cooked, it's better than the way we do it now. So much more casual and relaxed, with the radio on, the light streaming in through the French windows, her mother dressed and presentable, not sitting hunched in a bitter silence, or moping, or arguing about bridge . . . yes, above all, no bridge talk. No "Why can't you make a bid? You're sitting there with eleven points, that's eleven more than you might have, and you don't bid!" And then there was a scrabbling noise at the door, and in walked a very small tortoiseshell cat, head held proudly high, surveying the room and its occupants with a proprietorial air.

"Trixie!" Victoria leapt off her chair, scooped up the cat and clasped it to her with a fever of affection. The cat was not unwilling; it began placidly to nuzzle at Victoria's neck and to rub its head against her chin, deep, throbbing purrs vibrating throughout its entire body.

"Finish your breakfast, for heaven's sake," her mother said impatiently. "Why all this fuss over the cat all of a sudden? It's as if you hadn't seen her for a year."

More than that, you fool, thought Victoria, sitting down again resentfully, the cat still on her lap. She knew what these stupid idiots didn't know, that this adorable sweet-smelling affectionate playful little ball of fluff was shortly to be flattened *splat* under a Ford Cortina, was to become a patch of furry gore and squashed entrails right outside in the middle of Fairfax Road, oh-so-conveniently just in time for the Hadleys to move to a second floor flat where keeping a cat would have been impossible anyway. And there was nothing — not a single bloody thing that she could do about it. Trixie reached up, placed a paw on her shoulder and lifted her face to Victoria's for a cat-kiss.

"Well, I must be off," said Mr Hadley, rudely intruding, and

Mrs Hadley made some remarks to the effect that if Victoria could possibly tear herself away from the cat, a cat which had only been purchased on the understanding that Victoria would feed it, and a fine joke *that* had turned out to be . . . if the cat might be deposited on the floor where it belonged, perhaps they too might make a move.

Sullenly Victoria collected her things. She didn't want to go to school. She wanted to stay here, to play with Trixie, to poke about in the house and dig out all her old belongings. But there was no way out of it. Her father roared off in the car; she and her mother set off on foot in the opposite direction. Her mother had always accompanied her to the school gates, on the way to the High Street and the Building Society where she worked. Quite unnecessary, thought Victoria, sulking along two paces behind. And there it was: Fairfax Road Junior School, the very building in which she'd begun her formal education at the age of four and a half. You *heard* the school long before you turned the corner and came upon it — the shrill squealings, shriekings and screechings of two hundred children at play. Play? It sounded like a very serious affair. It sounded as if seventeen separate murders were taking place simultaneously. Had she ever made noises like that?

"Have a nice day," said her mother as they parted at the gate. Victoria did not return the sentiment. She was too busy working things out — what form she was in, where she should go. Of course, all she had to do was to find people whom she remembered as being in the same form as herself, and go along with them. There was that Rebecca Whatsit with the ginger hair, and her friend — what was she called? — Catherine. They looked absurdly young to be Victoria's contemporaries, though in fact she was even smaller than they. And how enormous the oldest boys and girls were — giants, none of them more than eleven. It was very confusing. Victoria prowled by the railings, trying to adjust to her size. She was standing at the edge of two apparently separate football games which every now and then collided, causing much chaos and an unspeakable row. Jumpers were laid down for goalposts, and a few feet away from her was a very small, weedy-looking goalkeeper, the epitome of the Last One to be Picked, looking extremely worried.

She had her time-scale worked out now. It was the hot summer, the year her mother stopped working, the year they moved, and therefore her last year at this school. So she must be in Miss Barrow's class, for that was the highest she'd reached. And it must be nearly the end of the summer term, so in fact she had not long to go. But the move had been a very sudden thing, it had all happened during the holidays, so nobody would know she was leaving. Miss Barrow's class — young, nice, pretty Miss Barrow. What a stir she, Victoria, could cause in the classroom, with her fifteen years of knowledge. With an inward chuckle she pictured Miss Barrow's face as she aired her knowledge of the Sine Rule, made passing reference to that beastly Jane Austen book they were doing for English Lit., described in detail the process of photosynthesis in green plants. It was going to be quite a day.

Some girls in a cluster by the school building were waving to her frantically. She recognized them as people she'd been friendly with, and began reluctantly to wander in their direction, skirting the football arena. The little goalkeeper had come to grief; he was flat out on the tarmac, his head bleeding copiously, while the opposition jeeringly rammed the ball past his helpless form twenty-one times, twenty-two, twenty-three . . .

More injury over by the side gate, where a girl of five or six was bawling her head off. A crowd had gathered around her and were hustling her towards the plump, elderly lady who had always patrolled the grounds at playtime, breaking up fights and mopping up blood. And then a bell rang and there was a roaring, savage charge for the doors. Victoria stood well back, taking it in. God, but you did have to be tough, when you were small. It was trample or be trampled.

But in the classroom they became almost civilized, sitting down at their desks without the slightest attempt to bang each other's heads on them, and Miss Barrow came in beaming all over her face, as if she actually liked them. For a moment Victoria couldn't remember where she'd sat, but then she saw the place — there in the middle row by that girl Maria Caldwell, who had a lovely dog called Sam, and a mentally retarded sister called Lynn who came home at weekends and wet herself at every possible

66

moment and destroyed the house. Maria Caldwell and Victoria had been very good friends, she remembered, but couldn't remember why.

The school day started dully; the usual Assembly. As she walked along the corridor Victoria was overwhelmed by the smell — it was a smell peculiar to Junior Schools, and she had quite forgotten it. It took her back as nothing else could — that smell that was disinfectant and chalk and soap and school dinner and medicated toilet paper, a smell that was trapped into the very fabric of the school, rubbed into its bones. It was strongest in the corridors, particularly near the toilets and the canteen, weakest in the classrooms. But wherever you went it was there.

Back in the classroom, Victoria found herself thinking in terms of "what lesson is it first today?" She had discovered for the first time in Assembly that it was a Friday. The clock seemed fond of Fridays. But of course it wasn't like that at Junior School — no packaging of the day into forty-minute sections, no trudging from Maths to French to Biology. Here, you had just the one teacher for almost everything, and there wouldn't be another bell till break. She remembered, now, how awesome she had found it at first at Secondary School, each subject being so massively complex that no teacher had mastered more than two of them, and most only one. That first day, when they'd been given their first year timetable! She had felt immensely important and knowledgeable simply to be the possessor of such a thing; to be confirmed, in writing, as a person who studied Chemistry, and Physics.

Here, much depended on Miss Barrow's whim. Her initial whim was to write on the blackboard a list of twenty words, which they were to copy into their spelling books and learn over the weekend. Maria had been chattering away — why had Victoria hung about on her own by the railings? Didn't she like them any more? "I was thinking about something," Victoria said vaguely, and Maria launched into a stream of gibberish about projects and Suzanne's sister and Sports Day and was it true about Mr Jackson, and Victoria said really, yes, no, probably. She found her spelling book and was confronted with her eight-year-old handwriting, large, wobbly and unformed, light years away from her current scrawl. She tried to imitate the old writing, for fun: "weight", "height", "breathe" right through to "restaurant" and "marriage", finishing way ahead of everyone else. "And get on with your Readers when you've finished," said Miss Barrow. Victoria found the Reader, a sadly dog-eared affair. She had no intention of reading it; instead, she looked around.

The classroom was a riot of colour; paintings, drawings, collages and charts were battling for space on every wall. She saw her own name on the most gruesome drawing of a house, a box of a house with a lollipop tree beside it, and, yes, a sun, a yellow blob with yellow rays spidering out. Art never had been her strong point. At the back of the room was a bookcase; at the front a large cupboard which she knew to contain paper, glue, scissors, paints, chalks, and a hundred and one things besides.

She could remember most of the children quite well now. There were a few whose names eluded her, which was daft — but then some people are so totally forgettable. There were very few to whom she had given a single thought since the day she had left the school. She saw Martin Bradshaw, he whose head she had so bloodily damaged, eyeing her furtively, as well he might. That revolting Howard Pitts with his constantly running nose, drip drip, drip like a faulty tap . . . always there was a pendulous grey globbet descending towards his mouth. What happened when it reached it? Yurk. And — good God – Cherry Grisholm. Victoria had forgotten all about the Grisholms. There were six or seven of them that she knew of, and quite possibly more; they all had pinched little faces with burning red cheeks and thin red lips; they wore clothes that looked like rejects from an Oxfam shop, they had mean tempers and they stank to the skies. They also had ridiculous names, names that didn't belong in the same family; apart from Cherry there were the twins, Sharon and Henry; Sean; Vernon; and Demelza, the smallest and smelliest Grisholm of all. What had happened to them? Cherry would be fifteen now, and probably pregnant; most of the others would be in Council Care, except for Sharon, who should, by rights, be in Borstal.

Sharon was the one Victoria remembered most vividly — eleven-year-old, knowing, vicious Sharon, who had loathed her, picked on her, sought her out in the play-group to threaten her.

And all because Victoria had once said something to Cherry about not coming near her again until she'd had a bath, if she knew what such a thing was. On the whole, Victoria had had an easy ride through junior school. She looked right. She had the looks of a Popular Girl, and could have been one had she worked at it, but she was too anti-social, and disliked too many people. Nonetheless, her appearance, her cool, confident air, had protected her from bullying; there were so many pale, quivering, nervous little victim-types around. Until Sharon started. Stupid though it seemed now, Victoria had been just a bit afraid of Sharon. Sharon was the person who'd really needed her head banged against a radiator, but unfortunately Victoria had never had the nerve. It would not have been wise, with a Grisholm. Well, if Sharon tried anything today, she was in for a small surprise. Thoughtfully, Victoria selected two of the fattest books she could find, and slipped them into her swimming bag.

"Don't forget, swimming after break," said Miss Barrow. "Take your kit with you and line up at the front gate as soon as the bell goes." Some school, this, thought Victoria; it'll be lunchtime when we get back, and all we'll have done all morning is to write down twenty words. She turned to Maria Caldwell, but Maria said haughtily: "I don't know what's wrong with you today, but if you're not speaking to us, then we're not speaking to you!" — this last with great triumph — and stalked off with Rebecca and Catherine. "Why, you fickle thing, you'll break my heart," muttered Victoria, in her Southern Belle voice. She herself was in no great hurry to go outside; the shrieking had already begun, the mob riot was under way. Where did they get the energy? The sun was blistering down by now, the classroom like a furnace. But outside they charged and yelled and bounded. Victoria decided to spend break in the toilets.

But when she got there she found them already occupied by none other than Sharon Grisholm, who was wiping her nose on the roller towel, fairly standard Grisholm behaviour. Sharon turned, and curled her lip. She was wearing a particularly hideous dress, a shapeless green nylon affair; the armpits dank with sweat.

"Well, look who it is," said Sharon, her voice heavy with

menace. "Little Miss Snotbag. What d'you want to do in there, then?" She jabbed her finger towards the row of toilet compartments. "You tell me what you want to do and I'll think about whether I'll let you do it. Miss Snotbag."

"You ought to know," said Victoria. "Your family seem to be experts on snot. You spray tons of it over the school every day. Wherever you go, you leave some behind you." It really felt good, saying that. It felt fantastic.

"*What* did you say?"

"I said, your entire family is a heap of festering excrement," said Victoria, "and you in particular are a putrefying warthog. Except," she added, "that warthogs smell better." Sharon's face purpled in rage and disbelief. I could kill her if I wanted to, thought Victoria. Presumably Sharon would be carted off to a mortuary, a pleasant enough thought, and no permanent damage would be done, as this day didn't exist — but the immediate consequences for herself would be awkward. The day would be ruined. And she didn't possess a lethal weapon anyway. So, as Sharon advanced with claws outstretched, ready for a good gouging, Victoria contented herself with swinging the swimming bag round sharply and clouting her a massive thwack in the face. Sharon reeled back, howling in agony. The corner of one of the books — such fine, sharp corners — had cut open the side of her nose. Her face would be one huge bruise by the evening. Victoria made a rapid exit, half alarmed, half excited at what she'd done. Felling a Grisholm! There was no danger that Sharon would go running to one of the teachers — that wasn't the Grisholm way. The Grisholm way was to get vengeance, with interest. They would wait their moment, wait till she was quite alone, and then the lot of them, big Sean, Vernon, Cherry, Henry, Demelza too for all she knew, would beat her to a pulp. Or so Sharon thought.

They were transported to the swimming baths in a nasty little Education Authority bus. Despite the broiling heat, Victoria wasn't looking forward to it. Swimming had never appealed to her — all that splashing around with her lovely hair imprisoned inside one of those hideous rubbery caps, and water getting up her nose. She had been pleased when compulsory school visits had ended after the second year at St. Catherine's.

And now it all came back to her, as she stood there at the side of the pool, cap gripping her skull, her bare toes wiggling. (Such small toes. It was hard to get used to them.) The clear, unnaturally blue water, with the thick black lines on the bottom of the pool wobbling and shimmering — the shrill, distorted noises echoing around, the whistles being blown, the powerful smell of chlorine. She remembered floundering in the learners' pool, moving on to the big pool, the first time she'd dared to jump in, her early attempts at diving. Diving had been what she liked best — much better than swimming up and down, up and down — your arms got tired, and it was dead boring anyway. The games teacher was busy with the non-swimmers, who were paddling around in the learners' pool, clinging to their floats for dear life. So Victoria spent the whole time amusing herself by diving off the springboard, under the close eye of one of those lifeguard people.

But the teacher must have seen her, for as they were lining up, damply bedraggled, ready for the drive back, she called Victoria out, her voice sharper than an icicle. Why hadn't Victoria told her she could dive? Why had she pretended that she couldn't? It was very stupid behaviour indeed, wasn't it? She was a silly little idiot. Well, if she could dive like that she could jolly well pull her socks up and represent Fairfax Road in the end-of-term swimming gala, have you got that, young lady? She would be entered in the Open Diving, and she had better win, that was all.

"Yes miss," said Victoria; for although she could say anything at all, although this was a golden opportunity to be as rude as she had ever wanted to be, she was hot, and she was tired, and she wasn't enjoying the day at all, and she simply couldn't be bothered. "Oh, go away," the teacher said crossly, as if she had been hoping for a row, and was further angered by such meek and instant submission.

The drive back to school was hot and uncomfortable, and the school dinner a none too pleasant fishy affair. When Miss Barrow announced that the afternoon was to be given over to practice for the school sports, it was the last straw. Running about with bean bags, eggs and spoons in this heat? Jumping and sprinting? They had to be joking. So much for Pythagoras and Jane Austen. This

71

was all a rotten waste of time. It hadn't gone at all the way she'd hoped; she just felt out of place, and very bored. Well, she'd had enough. She had her front door key; nobody would miss her out there in the scrummage, and if they did it was just too bad. Victoria was going home.

EIGHT

Remembered summers are always the warmest, and this one, surely, the warmest of all. The sun baked down relentlessly from a vivid unbroken blue expanse of sky, and there was not a breath of air to disturb the stillness; only a hazy shimmering, as if the world were quaking before the power of the heat. To Victoria, fresh from a damply capricious April, it was overpowering.

Slipping out unobserved through the side gate had been an easy affair; the entire school seemed to be turned out for the afternoon's exertions. The focus of attention was far away on the other side of the building, and nobody was looking her way at all. However, she could not go home by the direct route or she would certainly be seen — a detour around the park was called for. Possibly some busybody might point out her absence at some stage — Maria Caldwell, quite likely — but what could they do? They could phone her home; she wouldn't answer. They could even come round; still she wouldn't answer. She would be peacefully toasting herself in the back garden with a plentiful supply of iced lemon squash, and the cat for company. The neighbours were all out during the day, so there was little chance that anyone would see her. Even if they did, she could just say the school had the afternoon off.

It is interesting to walk along roads that you knew well seven years ago but haven't seen since. Victoria's mind was occupied with memories: so occupied that she was only three houses away by the time she noticed her father's car parked outside their gate. It was the very same car as they had nowadays, but wonderfully rejuvenated, shining and gleaming in the sun. Its presence was alarming. *Blast.* What was he doing home? And what was she to do? He might come out at any moment. She whirled around, looking for cover on the opposite side of the road, but there was nothing but the railings and hedge that formed the back of the park, with no entrance for two hundred yards. She crept closer, up to the wall which separated their garden from that of number 22. Until this point her view of their house had been obscured by the luxuriant summer growth of trees and bushes; only now could she see it, and there was no movement, nothing — the house looked empty. She saw her chance; there was room for her newly-diminutive form to slip into her old hiding-place, between the bushes by the side wall and the wall itself. She had spent hours in there as a child, throwing things at passers-by. It was a superb place; you were quite invisible. Five seconds later she had scrambled over the front wall and was hidden.

And not before time — for she had just made herself reasonably comfortable, and was beginning gloomily to wonder if this was to be the whole afternoon: her father in the house, and herself combating pins and needles and insects of every kind in a bush, when the front door opened, and she saw her father standing in the doorway. He stepped out, turned and said something inaudible, and then a girl came out. A pretty little thing of twenty or so, with dark curly hair. Before Victoria's astonished eyes she walked — no, scuttled — down the path behind Mr Hadley, saying: "One of these days your neighbours are going to be in, Simon — and then what?"

"Hurry up and get in the car, will you, Phil? It's ten past two already," was her father's irritated reply. He revved up the engine, and tapped impatiently on the steering wheel as the girl tripped round to the passenger side; even before she had closed her door they were shooting away, back towards St. John's Wood.

Victoria didn't move. For five full minutes she squatted there, as if afraid to come out into the open. She was shocked. She had thought herself so sophisticated. She tried to tell herself that it was nothing; that every self-respecting solicitor nipped back home with a girl while his wife was out, it went on all the time . . .

but when it was your own father, your own house, it was different. Stupid, incredibly stupid of her to get worked up about something that had happened seven years ago — but from what the girl had said it was by no means the first time, so why should it be the last? Victoria felt no particular emotion, not anger, not even disapproval — just overwhelming shock. It needed a lot of taking in.

She wriggled out of the bush, dragging the satchel behind her, and let herself into the house. She felt very much alone, the possessor of a dangerous secret. What should she do? She must think. She slapped together two enormous ham and cheese sandwiches, and took them out to the back garden, along with the long-awaited iced drink. The sun bed was comfortable enough, but there were wasps about, wasps who were interested in her sandwiches, and even more so in her iced lemon; she had to bolt them down, flapping away with her left hand, and being very careful not to bolt a wasp by mistake. Trixie was nowhere to be found.

The girl. Was she her father's secretary? It seemed likely. She couldn't actually remember there having been one called Phil, but then her father had never talked much about his work. She had been quite old before she had any real idea of what he did. She knew that the current secretary was called Joyce, but then Joyce had been in residence for a few years now. Really, he had some nerve! Her mother's place of work was less than half a mile away, and though she was known to lunch regularly at the health food restaurant in the High Street with her office friend Sarah, surely the risk was enormous. They could so easily be seen in the car! Didn't he care? Well — when had her father ever cared about anything, except that trumps broke well and the club finesse was working and his partner didn't botch his brilliantly conceived defence?

But the heat was so enervating that even thinking was far too strenuous an occupation. Her brain didn't have the energy. There was plenty of time . . . she would work it out later . . . and then she must have dozed off, for suddenly her mother appeared, looking cross and over-heated, and said:

"Really, Victoria, lying in the direct heat on a day like this! Do

75

you want sunstroke? You'd be much more comfortable over there in the shade. Move, now."

Do you know? wondered Victoria. No, you don't. Obviously you don't know.

"I'm making salad for tea; cold meat and salad. I couldn't bear it in the kitchen with the oven on. What a summer this is! If the weather doesn't break soon I think I'll melt. A good thunderstorm . . ."

You don't know, thought Victoria, and trotted into the house after her; this jaded, tired mother was far more what she was used to. Now, what to do? She would wait until her father got home. He might, just might, have an explanation; might mention that he had to drop in at lunchtime to fetch something — but with his secretary? No. Victoria wasn't that green. "One of these days your neighbours will be at home, Simon . . ."

He had nothing to say. He put his case down, and smiled hello at Victoria, who was lying flat out on the sofa, stroking Trixie and watching TV. The cat had miraculously reappeared on the dot of feeding time, nosing her way daintily into the kitchen at the very moment that the can opener punctured the rabbit flavour Kittomunch. Mr Hadley said whew, wasn't it hot? — and had they had a good day? He himself had had a pretty dull one. Indeed, thought Victoria, eyeing him with dislike, and what do you get up to on the exciting ones? Dance naked around the Round Pond?

The salad was a fair example of her mother's culinary talent: quartered, withered-looking tomatoes nestling amongst leaves of limp, pale yellow lettuce, mountains of thick, uninviting white cabbage, undersized radishes, not very well washed, and a bottle of salad cream to wash it down with. Glumly Victoria took her seat at the table. She wasn't going to enjoy this one bit. Rabbit food was for rabbits, and she was finding it very hard to look her father in the eye. The rotten creep!

"Will you be playing bridge tonight, do you think?" her mother asked.

"I should think I'll wander in for a few hours a bit later," said her father, spearing a radish with an expression of pained resignation.

76

Times had indeed changed, if it was necessary to ask such a question. But then, when she was young he hadn't played every night, not by any means; she could remember him sitting there on numerous occasions, watching some awful news or current affairs programme, and herself sulking because she wanted the other channel. And as for her mother — while they were living at Fairfax Road her mother had played bridge only once in a blue moon. It had meant a baby sitter, and Victoria was not known for her kindness to baby sitters. Very seldom had any of them returned for a second stint. They'd always been teenage girls . . . there was that one who had chattered away so foolishly to Victoria about how she was a vegetarian, how meat absolutely made her *cringe*. It turned her stomach upside down. How could people murder poor little animals and eat them? Victoria had sat downstairs until ten thirty, curled up in the armchair with a chicken carcass on her lap, tearing pieces off and gnawing greasily, with an occasional doleful "cluck cluck". She had scared off one particularly nervous one by wandering round the house wearing nothing but her socks; the stupid nurd hadn't known where to look, and Victoria was only six at the time! Any babysitter reckless enough to use the Hadley's phone would soon hear a small voice calling down the stairs: "That'll be forty-five pence, please. I timed you." No, her mother hadn't got much bridge in in those days — but then it hadn't seemed to matter to her, it wasn't the driving force that it was now. Only after they'd moved had the bug really started to bite.

Suddenly Victoria caught her own name, and became aware that she was being discussed.

". . . so quiet today!" her mother was saying. "There — she didn't even hear that! Are you all right, Victoria?"

"I'm fine."

"But you really do seem odd. It must be the weather. You've hardly said a word all day — and when you do, you aren't talking the way you usually talk."

This was unexpectedly observant of her. Victoria had taken pains not to use words that might seem suspiciously advanced for a child of eight, and yet her mother had noticed. Of course, speech does change in other ways, more subtle, less obvious: you adopt fashionable words, copy from other people expressions of which you like the sound, use phrases that catch your fancy, almost to saturation point, and then drop them like a brick — but she would have thought her mother too vague, too uninterested, to discern any difference.

"And you haven't said a word about school today. You always come home full of what's happened during the day."

Had she truly been such a loquacious little bore? Well, she could hardly say: "I smashed Sharon Grisholm's face in and then I bunked off for the afternoon" — so she just said something vague to the effect that it had all been very dull: swimming, singing, and then the sports all afternoon.

"That doesn't sound dull. It sounds like great fun. Are you in the relay this year, or the hundred metres, or the jumping?"

"Yes," said Victoria, and her mother sighed.

"You see what I mean, Simon? She's definitely off colour."

"I hadn't noticed anything," said her father, thereby surprising nobody, and then, thankfully, the meal broke up, large amounts of white cabbage remaining to be consigned to the dustbin.

Mr Hadley, freshly clad in clean shirt and light jacket, departed for the bridge club shortly afterwards. If, indeed, he was going to the club, thought Victoria — how could you trust him, how could you tell? She had decided that she must tell her mother. In some ways it seemed pointless; it was really an illusion that she had a momentous secret to impart. The main line mother, the one who had reached 1983, wouldn't know — unless she had found out for herself. This was the crux of it. Victoria was certain that she had found out, so careless was her father, so marked the change in her mother after the summer of 1976. So to tell her now would do no lasting damage, would alter nothing — except that it might well provide Victoria with some information, give her some clues. There was bound to be a confrontation, probably a big scene, a real shouting match. She was only precipitating something that must have happened anyway.

But none of this rationalization could make it an easy thing to do. For more than two hours she put it off, while her mother made a half-hearted attempt to clear the chaos that was the sitting-room, had a bath and emerged in a cotton dressing-gown;

78

while she herself did the same, while they watched a slightly better than average sit-com on TV. Her mother said some things that made sense to her, and others, about Gran's last letter, and a programme they'd watched last night, and someone called Lucy, which didn't. Her silence on these topics reinforced her mother's belief that she wasn't quite herself — how true — and she had to swallow a vitamin pill. The nine o'clock news came and went, a montage of flashback, images of Harold Wilson, Prime Minister, of Margaret Thatcher, Leader of the Opposition, of Jimmy Carter, President of the United States . . . strange to think that she alone in the world knew the future fortunes of these people, only one of whom would be a figure of importance by 1983. She knew who the next American President would be, and that he would survive an assassin's bullet. Ditto the Pope. She knew that John Lennon would be murdered and that Elvis Presley would die. She could tell her mother all these things, and it would make no difference; she would just say "How morbid you are, Victoria", and give her another pill, or become alarmed at her daughter's sudden precocious political awareness. And Victoria had something else to tell her. *Now.* Do it now.

"Mum?"

"Yes?" Mrs Hadley shifted slightly in her chair, comfortable in her innocence. She was reading a library copy of *Cancer Ward*.

"Why . . ." oh-so-casually, scrutinizing her own left hand with apparent fascination . . . "why was Dad home at lunchtime?"

"Was he? I've no idea why. I expect he forgot something. How do you know, anyway?"

"We drove past in the bus coming home from swimming," said Victoria, "and I saw him come out to the car and drive off. I don't know who the girl was, though."

There was suddenly a change in the atmosphere: a darkening, a crackling of danger. And then her mother said, slowly, deliberately:

"What girl was that, Victoria?"

"The one he was with. I just wondered, that's all. It doesn't matter." Oh dear. Perhaps this wasn't such a clever idea after all. Her mother's face had frozen into a death-mask.

"No, it doesn't matter," she said, in a voice so unnaturally brittle, so high and false and agonized, that it made Victoria's head hurt. There followed a couple of minutes of silence, heavy with strain; minutes during which Victoria thought, "Is she going to sit there like that all night, or what?" and "No, it really wasn't worth it, I should have known that," and Mrs Hadley's face drained to grey, clenched into a tight little ball of misery. "Say something," thought Victoria, "for God's sake say something, or do something, this is so bloody embarrassing . . ."

And still she said nothing, and Victoria could bear it no longer. A real girl of eight would have said something already, asked what was wrong. It was as if she had given herself away; as if her own unchildlike silence were proof of guilt, of complicity. Muttering: "I think I'll go to bed, then," she got up and left the room. Her mother didn't seem to notice; before Victoria was halfway up the stairs she heard her start to cry. No soft weeping this, but hoarse, painful, tearing sobs, a grief so violent, so intense that Victoria couldn't begin to comprehend it, and it frightened her. Damn you! she thought, slamming her bedroom door. She couldn't stand the noise; it cut through her, made her shudder, like the sound of fingernails scraping down a blackboard. How could she sit and cry? Why didn't she *do* something? Howling away like that, making Victoria feel bad — oh, it had all gone wrong. It was a catastrophe. She stuffed cotton wool into her ears, and almost at once took it out again, for her father might come home, or her mother take it into her head to phone him, and she must be able to hear. Trixie scratched at the door in a frenzy.

"You," Victoria said unhappily to the cat, "are the only good thing about this whole day." Perhaps it was wisest not to tamper with things you didn't fully understand, not to play dangerous games — but it hadn't seemed to be dangerous. It was just an experiment. Down below the crying had stopped, leaving a silence like a living thing sliding its tentacles through the house. Victoria tiptoed down the first five stairs and, peeking over the banisters, saw the shape of her mother, still huddled in the chair. The book had fallen to the floor, and with her left hand she was picking at the fabric of the chair arm, pulling out threads, pulling, pulling, as if this was a task of great urgency that had been set her: the chair must be unravelled. Victoria went back to her room. It looked as if her mother wouldn't be moving from that chair until her father came home. There was nothing she could do for the present.

And suddenly she wanted Daniel, wanted him more desperately than she had wanted anything in her life. But the Daniel she wanted didn't exist; there was only a boy of eleven, to whom the name Victoria Hadley meant nothing. But all the same — a boy of eleven — what had he been like, wondered Victoria, seizing with relief upon this new train of thought, this distraction from her mother downstairs. Yes — that's what she *should* have done today. Caught a bus to Daniel's home — he had lived his whole life in the same semi-detached house — waited outside until he came home from school, stopped him, spoken to him — surely he would have seen that she was something special, although it was six years too early. Something would have clicked; he would have known it to be a meeting of great importance. Wouldn't he? Knowing that it was madness — what did it matter? — she went into her parents' room, picked up the telephone extension, that extension on which she had so gleefully eavesdropped on the babysitters' phone calls to their boyfriends, and dialled Daniel's number.

"7432 — who's speaking?"

Well, well. The old cretin himself. And what a charming telephone manner he had. "I'd like to speak to Daniel," she said.

"He's not available, and I've asked you once: who's that speaking? I want to know!"

"I bet you do, you old monster." For so long now she'd wanted to tell Mr Priestley what she thought of him. She would probably never have another chance. "Your children can't breathe, let alone receive phone calls, without you knowing all the details. What business is it of yours who I am? You're the king of all the turds of all the toads in the world!"

"I beg your pardon!" roared Mr Priestley, and Victoria said, with grim enjoyment:

"Oh, don't apologize; it's so painful to hear a man grovel" and hung up. Oh well. Daniel at eleven would probably have been a severe disappointment anyway, a skinny little boy with sticking-

81

out ears and a quavery unbroken voice . . . but all the same, it would have been such a remarkable thing to see him. Maybe another time — although the way she was feeling right now, it would be a long time before she messed around with the clock again.

No change downstairs. It was starting to get boring. There was nothing to do. She was surrounded by a child's paradise of toys, books and games, all quite useless to her now. She began to rummage through her satchel, found her old English exercise book, and read through it with wry amusement, wincing at the spelling, and at the banality of the story-lines. She had, at this stage of her life, been suffering from a multiple-birth fetish. Every story began in the same way: "Jane and Lucy were twins . . ." "Hurry up," said mother to the triplets . . ." and finally, in a story written only a fortnight before: "Sarah, Michael, Laura and Robin were quads . . ."

The front door banged. Victoria stiffened with nervousness, and slipped cautiously out on to the landing. Her father was saying ". . . absolutely atrocious . . . I've never seen anything like it. First he goes off in a lay down vulnerable slam . . ." Her mother said something inaudible, and then they closed the door, and their voices could be heard only as a faint buzzing. It was puzzling — for all the world as if nothing had happened. Victoria began to slither down the stairs, and promptly had to bolt back into her room, as her father came out again, upstairs and into the lavatory. She waited for the flush and the sound of his footsteps receding down the stairs, and then returned to her post. For ten minutes she sat there, wondering and waiting, and another ten, and still nothing happened, or not that she could hear. The cat padded over and sat beside her, purring throatily. And then at last her vigilance was rewarded; the voices rose, her father's cross, abrupt and impatient, her mother's with a note of hysteria. Victoria heard things said that night the like of which she had never imagined. Her mother, pleading pathetically, laying herself open; her father retorting cruelly, until finally he said:

"I'm fed up to the back teeth with all this over-dramatizing. If you don't like it then say the word and I'll move out tomorrow. It's up to you. I don't honestly care either way." His voice was one of boredom; of total indifference, the cruellest thing of all. The bastard! Tell him to get out, Victoria screamed silently, tell him to go this minute, you never want to see the stinker again — but her mother just sobbed: "I don't want you to go, I never want you to go."

"All right, then, I'll stay. Now, what about some coffee? I've had the most appalling evening . . ."

"What about me? What sort of an evening do you think I've had, sitting here thinking about . . ."

"Oh, don't start again, for God's sake. You're getting on my nerves. Look — I've admitted it, I've told you the truth, I've offered to leave but no, that doesn't suit you, so I've agreed to stay. What more do you want from me?"

"Yes, stay — and carry on like this, that's what you mean. Well, you shan't. I'm going to leave my job. I'll give my notice in on Monday." Her voice was lower now, more controlled. "An then *I'll* be here all day, so you can take your bloody little typist anywhere you want but at least I'll know that you haven't had her here in my house — in my home."

"You do whatever you want, Pat. It's your problem. Now, unless you've got anything more to say, I think I'll . . ."

Victoria heard no more. She stumbled back to her room and buried her head in the bedclothes, seething with hatred, hatred not for her father but for her mother, for being such a hopeless, despicable wretch, for allowing herself to be demeaned, for having no pride — for choosing a life that was to become little more than mere existence, in order to hang on to someone who humiliated her and cared nothing for her. Victoria felt contaminated, as if a poison were seeping through the entire household. For many more hours she lay awake, with only the cat for comfort; her last conscious thought was that it would have been a much better thing if it had been her parents who were killed by the Ford Cortina, and the cat who had lived.

NINE

The clock behaved immaculately, returning Victoria to 1983 at precisely the point at which she had left it. But the memories of that scorching summer day with its dark, stormy undertones were to linger stubbornly on, as the months passed and spring gave way to summer. The June exams ended and were followed by a riot of end-of-term fun and frivolity, but Victoria was dead to it all. She was haunted by her glimpse of the truth behind her parents' marriage. It was like discovering that she was living in a house that was riddled with disease.

Why she should mind so much she didn't know. She had always felt far removed from her parents, untouched by anything they said or did. They had been patently uninterested in her, so it would have been very foolish to take any interest in them. And now, unwittingly, they had begun to affect her. She found their company, her mother's in particular, unbearably oppressive. Such were Victoria's contempt and disgust for her that she could hardly bring herself to speak to her. She knew now how things had happened. Some time during that freak summer her mother had found out about Phil — it wouldn't have been very difficult — and given up work, all just as she had heard it. She also suspected that this was in some way linked to their move to the flat in Ladbroke Grove, though the nature of the link wasn't clear. Could it be that her mother, unable to live with what she saw as the desecration of her home, had demanded the change? Unlikely — for even had her father given way, why wouldn't they have bought another nice house? Why that claustrophobic little three-roomed flat?

She told it all to Daniel — she had to tell him. They were

sitting on a bench, in a secluded corner of the park which had become their special place for that summer. Daniel was appalled. Not by her mother's behaviour — for her he had nothing but sympathy — but by her father's.

"What an unbelievable way to treat anybody! How can people do such things? Your *poor* mother." Victoria could summon up no pity for her mother, and wasn't much inclined to try. She had chosen to stick it. It had been her own free decision. She could remember when she had felt sorry for Daniel's mother, that humble self-effacing victim of tyranny — but a voluntary victim. She wasn't sorry for her now. The bad old days when women were non-persons, forced to be dependent on their menfolk, were long gone, so what was wrong with people who'd choose to endure an unhappy life, an obviously disastrous marriage, rather than pack their things and clear out? Of course there was that bunk about putting up with it for the sake of the children — as if the offspring of a bad alliance were supposed mysteriously to benefit from the daily witnessing of the bad alliance in action. That certainly wasn't relevant in her mother's case. Did her sex have some deep, ineradicable instinct for masochism? Was that the answer? It was a sinister and deeply depressing thought.

". . . so very sorry, Victoria," Daniel was saying. "It must be terrible for you, really terrible. How on earth did you find out?"

"I overheard them arguing about it," said Victoria, sucking on her ice lolly. Lollies were a childish thing, but she was inordinately fond of them, as long as they didn't touch her teeth, which was agonizing. Daniel was a choc-ice man. "They didn't mean me to hear, obviously, but the walls are so thin in our flat." She still couldn't find the words to explain about the clock. Adultery was so much simpler than time machines.

"But," said Daniel, hesitantly — "If . . . if that's how he feels about her, why did he marry her? If you don't mind my asking."

"Because I was on the way," said Victoria. She had looked through her mother's papers one evening while they were out playing bridge, found their marriage certificate, seen the date on it and drawn her own conclusions. "No wonder they never kept their wedding anniversary. Just think of everyone, looking at me and furtively counting on their fingers. So you could say I'm responsible for the whole mess. I botched their lives up well and truly."

"Well, I'm glad he had the decency to marry her at least," said Daniel, in no doubt as to what was the right thing to do. "But, Victoria, you can't blame yourself. It's nothing at all to do with you . . ."

"But I have to live with them, every bloody day — and I can't stand to be *near* them, Daniel, they're my bloody parents and just look at them — for years now they've been living like this and I hate it and I hate them and I can't get away!"

"Victoria," said Daniel — and then all of a sudden Daniel, to whom touching another human being was like scaling the Eiger, had put his arms right round her and was hugging her, with gentle unintelligible noises of consolation. And Victoria, who scorned tears, who thought that to shed them in public was the ultimate in feebleness, began to cry. And for the first time she knew that crying was exactly the right thing to do. Daniel expected it of her, even wanted it of her, so that he could do his bit properly — and after all, the longer she cried the longer they could sit here like this, which was very nice. Daniel — and now she began to cry in earnest, sobbing with all the frustration of being only fifteen, of having no say in anything, of having to live with her parents when the only person in the world with whom she wanted to be was Daniel. She thought bitterly how different the days would be, life would be, if each evening she could go back, not to *them*, but to him — and here they were, stuck with their rotten families, and not a thing could they do about it.

"Please don't be so unhappy, Victoria. I can't bear you to be so unhappy. I don't know what to say to you." His face was wrinkled into a frown of worry and concern, and it made him look so gorgeous, so absolutely edible, that she almost began to cry all over again. "Victoria, listen — when did you find out all this? Have you known for long?"

"Oh — since April," Victoria said, sniffling rather pleasurably with the sense of relief and release that comes with the aftermath of a four-star howl.

"I don't believe it. All through the exams you've had this on your mind? Why didn't you tell me sooner?"

"Well — your exams were much more important. And I hardly saw you, anyway."

"You should have told me. Some things are more important than any exam. It wouldn't have made any difference, anyway. I know I failed everything."

"You," said Victoria, "do not know *how* to fail an exam. It's a skill you were born without. You could have done nothing but play snakes and ladders from December till June and you'd have got into Cambridge just the same."

"And I'd be bloody good at snakes and ladders," said Daniel. He was only just mastering the art of swearing with conviction, and "bloody" was as far as he would go. Victoria's choicer morsels of profanity had shocked him rigid; he had implored her to abandon them, but to no avail. "I'd be the champion of the world. To think I've been wasting my time, revising . . ." He frowned. "My father, though — he still expects me to go to Cambridge. He sort of assumes I'm going."

"You haven't told him yet, then, that you want to stay in London." Mr Priestley ought to be pickled. The last thing she needed, now, was for Daniel to disappear.

"No — not yet. It's going to be very awkward, you know — there'll be an awful row . . . I'm not looking forward to it. No need to say anything until I have to. I mightn't get good enough grades for Cambridge."

"You will. You know you will."

"You don't believe I'm going through with it, do you?" asked Daniel, his face dark and brooding. "I can tell you don't. Well, you're wrong. Just you wait and see."

No, I'm not wrong, thought Victoria. Maybe you will find the courage to say your bit, but it will be about as effective as a butterfly against a bulldozer. But she said nothing. Daniel seemed to believe that he would emerge victorious from the confrontation, and even that represented quite a step forward. It wasn't for Victoria to douse him with cold water.

"There's something else I wanted to talk to you about," she said, and he nodded expectantly. "It'll sound odd, but it has been puzzling me. It's about my father. Solicitors earn good money, wouldn't you say?"

"I'm sure they do. It's one of the things my father wouldn't have minded me being."

"Yes. Well, in that case, I'd like to know where all my father's money goes. I've been thinking, and it just doesn't add up. When I was eight, we lived in a house like yours: nice area, garden. We'd had a new car the year before. Then all of a sudden they sold the house and we went to live in a grotty flat. Nowadays we live in a slightly less grotty flat. We still have the same car. We never go on holiday — in the old days we went every year, France mostly. Not now. My mother never seems to buy new clothes. They never buy anything! All our stuff is old. You know our flat. The television's terminally ill, the springs are going in the chairs, the cooker's got senile dementia."

"Yes, but *you* always seem to have lots of new things. They spend plenty on presents for you."

"I know that, I know a lot gets spent on me. That's their guilt money. I've known that for years. They buy me stuff to ease their consciences. I know it and they know I know it. But that doesn't begin to account for the money."

Daniel considered the problem. "You say that everything changed when you moved. Well, wasn't it about then that your mother stopped working? Of course there'd have been less money. Suddenly you were living on one income instead of two. Isn't that obvious?"

"Not to me. Her income was peanuts compared to his; it couldn't possibly have made such a dramatic difference. They'd have had to cut back a bit, yes, but not to the extent of selling the house. I don't count her money. I want to know about *his*. *Now*. What does he do with it all?"

"Well, the way he treats your mother ... I wouldn't be surprised if he just gives her the bare minimum to live on, and — I don't know, hoards the rest away somewhere for himself."

"Not him. Give him credit for that — he's not mean. Or perhaps I should say he's not particularly interested in money, otherwise I make it sound like a virtue. It's easy to be generous with something you're not interested in. He's interested in himself, and he's a miser with himself. Anyway, I've seen his bank statements floating around with all the other muck in the sitting-room. They aren't exactly enormous."

"Perhaps. It wasn't a very brilliant idea. What about bridge though? He's always playing bridge at this club, your mother too — surely it must cost a fortune to play there every night? Isn't there an entrance fee?"

"Table money, if you please," said Victoria. "Yes, it costs three pounds a time to play. I suppose that does add up, though it doesn't sound to me as if it would eat too big a hole in what a solicitor should be earning. But actually it costs him nothing to play, because — give him credit for this, too — he's a good player, and he's playing for money. He wins far more than he forks out in table money. Easily enough to cover my mother as well, and still make a profit."

"Isn't she a good player, then?"

"According to my father," Victoria said coldly, "she plays bridge with all the subtlety and talent of a haemorrhoid. I think she's actually about average for the circle she moves in."

"It's a good thing, you know, that she's got that one interest. At least while there's that she's going somewhere, meeting people — she hasn't copped out of life altogether."

"Unless she just goes along to keep an eye on *him*, make sure he's not slipping off to play strip poker with the barmaid. I think that probably is why she started going along with him so often. And then it got to be the game itself. It's certainly got a proper hold on her now."

"So she's got two good reasons for going. If you think about it, an intelligent woman like that, sitting around all day with no mental stimulation at all — it's not surprising she's become so hooked on bridge. It's a very complicated game, isn't it? I've seen the articles in the Sunday papers. It's probably the one thing that's kept her brain working at all. Now we've wandered off the point. Your father's money. Not bridge, then . . . oh, I can't think. Would he be giving it away to charity?"

"Oh dear — I really have given you the wrong impression. He's not *that* sort of generous. He wouldn't go without a new car just to feed the starving millions. Oh, it's no good, Daniel. You can't possibly understand why it seems so mysterious to me without knowing a lot more about my father."

Daniel shook his head in despair, shifted on the seat and kicked at a twig. "Well, then the only answer is that he's got another girlfriend now, and he's spending it all on her." He clapped his hand over his mouth. "Oh, no — Victoria, I didn't mean that. I . . ."

"Why not? Don't get worked up. I'm not going to care. I've got it out of my system for the time being. That's actually rather a clever idea. That he would be capable of." And strangely enough the thought didn't disturb her at all; it was as if it had been dancing along the borders of her subconscious for some time, just awaiting the opportunity to make itself known. But then, the fresh air, the sun, the quiet of the park, and most of all Daniel there beside her, were acting as anaesthesia. What it would feel like later, back in the mortuary atmosphere of her home, she couldn't know.

But Daniel's theory, plausible enough on the surface, fell apart under closer examination. Maybe her father was seeing a girl — that wouldn't be at all surprising — but when? It could only be brief encounters between appointments during his working day, or on the rare occasions when he went alone to the bridge club. Nothing so casual, so infrequent, would justify such a huge, regular expenditure. *Regular* — that was the thing. There was *never* money to spare. Lurid thoughts of blackmail flooded into her mind. But who? How? *Why*? "Pay up, or I'll tell your wife about your girlfriend"? Hardly. "Go ahead," he'd say with that sneering laugh of his. He wouldn't care.

More and more Victoria found herself retreating into her dreams of escaping from him to live with Daniel. Next year she would be sixteen. Couldn't you marry at sixteen? She wasn't sure that she actually wanted to *marry* Daniel, but it might be the only way. They could run away and be married on her next birthday, and by the time everyone found out it would be too late to stop them. People always said it was a terrible mistake to marry so young, but what did they know. Every rule has its exceptions. She and Daniel understood each other; they'd be all right. But by the time her next birthday came round — March — Daniel would in all probability be settled at Cambridge. It would interfere, too, with her own education, her career prospects. She couldn't somehow imagine herself being allowed back to school as Mrs Priestley, sporting her wedding ring. (No jewellery shall be worn by any girl.)

And so it looked as if it must wait until she left — three whole years more. By that time Daniel might be studying still, or might be working. It didn't matter. They could get a little place together, and Victoria would do Biology at university just as planned, and she need never see her parents again. She would cook fantastic meals every evening, and they would invite carefully selected friends round, friends who would go into paroxysms of envy. The flat would always be clean and tidy, no papers strewn over the furniture, no fat congealing on the cooker, no piles of bridge books on the floor. Maybe they would marry, maybe not; from what Victoria could see, marriage was not the most successful of arrangements. Anyway, for herself and Daniel it would be irrelevant. As long as they were together, it would be paradise. But three years was a lifetime away, a lifetime of parents and parents' flat and Daniel away in Cambridge. How could she wait three years? How could she bear it?

She didn't have to wait. She had a clock, a clock with a dial that went all the way to twenty-four. By now she had lost all her old fears of the clock; she had a good knowledge, if not understanding, of its behaviour. It sat innocently on her bedside table. So remarkable was the secret they shared that Victoria had come to think of it almost as a fellow-conspirator. Of course, just because it could take her back in time there was no reason to believe that it could take her forward. That *would* be incredible. It made a trip back to 1976 seem an absolute doddle by comparison. Taking her to a time that hadn't happened yet . . . how could it do that? Probably the higher numbers were for when you got older; when you were forty, fifty, and wanted to recapture for one brief day your golden youth. If she were to set the dial for, say, twenty, nothing would happen. Nevertheless, she was reluctant to try. Just in case. To wake up five years on, in a place you didn't recognize; to find yourself with people who knew you well but whom you had never met; to have no idea of what was happening in your life, where you should go, what you should do — it would be all but impossible to cope with. And yet. Such a unique chance. The sneak preview of all time. It could be very exciting. And yet . . .

She continued to argue with herself for several weeks, looking at the little white dial and looking away. Eventually she created a diversion by winding the key and setting the dial for quarter past one; a diversion which turned out to be much the nicest of her days in the past.

It began alarmingly; she awoke to find herself in a completely strange room, and, worse, in a cage. She sat up — or, rather, she tried to sit up, but her limbs weren't working properly, and she flopped down again, an undignified chubby ball. On her next attempt she made it, by clinging monkey-like to the cage bars — the cage, she now saw, was a large cot of some antiquity. There was a catch on the top to release the side. Victoria hauled herself to her feet, and promptly collapsed again as her legs gave way underneath her. She gritted her teeth and tried again — at least she had teeth, though not all that many by the feel of it. Her whole mouth seemed to have been transplanted from some-body else. She clung to the bars with a vice-like grip — no wonder babies needed so much sleep, it was obviously a most exhausting life — and this time her legs, though wobbly, held. Even releasing the catch was a tiresome, laborious exercise, for the tiny chubby pink fingers weren't used to such fiddly tasks. But she managed it, and heaved the side down with a triumphant bang.

Almost immediately she began to regret it. It was such a long way down to the floor that she was quite afraid of falling out. She was so small. She knew she must be small, because everything else was so big. She felt like a stray Lilliputian, or climber of beanstalks, helpless in the giant's den. The wardrobe in the opposite corner towered massively over her, while all around lurked monster cupboards and chairs. The only thing that was the proper size was herself, and even then she didn't feel quite right — as if she had been taken apart, redistributed and put back together in all the wrong proportions. Her head felt too big for her body. She couldn't actually see the body, for the vast majority of it was neatly zipped away inside a fluffy yellow sleeping-suit. It even covered her feet, which was a bit much. All

92

she could see was her hands, which were much softer, more delicate and unused-looking than they were to become. But they felt not at all alien — they were nice enough hands, and she was, after all, inside the body they were attached to. It was her mouth that was worrying; you get very used to the feel of the inside of your mouth. Your tongue spends so much time exploring it. But, on the whole, it was not herself, but the things around her that made her feel uncomfortable. Even the clock had tripled in size. It was . . . oh, hell's *bells!* The clock! How could she hide it this time? The short and simple answer was that she couldn't. And at any moment her mother would walk in, and . . .

The door clicked open, and in walked Victoria's grandmother.

"I heard a noise, darling; are you — oh, you naughty girl!" She came over to the opened cot and gently lifted Victoria out. "You undid your cot all by yourself? No, not clever. Very bad."

"Goo," said Victoria, and sucked her thumb. Gran? Why Gran? Were they staying with her? One thing was clear, and a great relief it was: Gran could neither see nor hear the clock. It was only inches away from her left elbow, and she was behaving as if it didn't exist. It was really some clock. No sooner had you become accustomed to one impossible aspect of its behaviour than it produced another. A few months ago she would have scorned the idea of invisibility; now it seemed positively run of the mill. Yes — but why Gran? Not that Victoria was complaining. Gran was wide awake and calm and cool and cheerful — a very far cry from an early-morning mother, scratchy, snappy, irritable, half asleep. Victoria liked her Gran.

"Have to get another catch fixed on there," said Gran. "We can't have you falling out, can we?"

"Gwan," said Victoria; there were so many questions she wanted to ask, but Gran would probably faint with shock if she tried. She was becoming aware of some layers of padding underneath the sleeping-suit, which just had to be a nappy. It could have been worse; at least it was dry. And so it would stay. Gran would have a nice surprise today: Victoria would be toilet trained.

Gran took off the sleeping-suit, checked the nappy — "What a good girl! Dry!" — and dressed her in a little embroidered cotton

93

frock. Still there was no sign of either of her parents, and it was beginning to seem that Victoria was here without them. Well, it was summer — early summer 1969 was when she'd set the clock for, and they must have gone on holiday and left her with Gran. What very good timing. A day away from her parents was exactly what Victoria needed.

And she enjoyed every minute of it. She had half-expected to be bored, sitting around all day in a pushchair saying "go ga goo" — but it wasn't like that at all. Being fifteen months old took a lot of concentration. Also, it was a very real part of her life, but one of which she had no memory, and this glimpse of the early Victoria was fascinating. Of course, it wasn't a typical day, because she was staying with Gran, but that was all the better. It was so peaceful, so restful to be away from her parents, not to have to watch their wordless battles, or listen to the arguments that came out on to the surface, the ones about bridge — to escape the daily misery of living with a bad partnership who had been dealt all the wrong cards.

She had thought that she didn't know this house, but as she was carried around, from bedroom to bathroom, downstairs and into the kitchen, it began to seem distantly familiar. She didn't remember anything until she saw it, but the moment she did she knew that it was *right*, that there was no other way it could possibly have been. What a good memory she must have. The bath just there, on the right as you went in, the rim brightly decked with plastic toys. The kitchen with the big boiler making whooshing noises in the corner by the door — surely she remembered that? And there was her high chair at the table, with a row of beads along the front and a bright yellow teddy-bear picture on the back.

"Eggies!" said Gran. There wasn't a lot you could say to eggies, so Victoria didn't. And so the day passed. Victoria was fed and changed and plonked on potties and re-fed and re-plonked. She was put out into the garden in a sun-bonnet; she was wheeled to the shops and to the park. She didn't recognize the neighbourhood, but it was clearly London — the big red double-decker buses were charging about all over the place. At one point she caught a glimpse of the river, but the only other

94

help she got was from a sign, which pointed the way to Putney. Victoria's knowledge of south London was too scanty to make anything of this at all.

The day had its low spots. Chief amongst them was the woman who visited Gran in the morning. Victoria was parked in the pram in the back garden, but she heard the voices quite clearly: Gran, rather wearily — "Can I get you a cup of tea, Madge?" and then — "That would be absolutely lovely, Dorothy, but first I must pop out and say hello to the little pumpkin!"

"Oh, nuts," thought Victoria, and pulled the blanket over her face. All too soon it was yanked down again, and an enormous heavily made-up face with prominent eyes, a wart on the cheek looking very much like a baked bean, and teeth that were brown around the edges, appeared only inches away from Victoria's own. A finger began to poke her in the cheek; Victoria wrinkled her nose in disapproval. The woman opened her mouth, blasting out a sickly stale smell, the smell of food which has been lingering in the cavities of the teeth for many days, blended with the aromas of a suppurating abscess in the gum and recently inhaled Consulate menthol cigarette. Out of the mouth, along with the smell, came the following remarkable statement: "Itchy cootchy bootchy dickle Vicky dicky dumdums!" Victoria gasped for air. "Bubsy wubsy pickles poo give Auntie Madgey a big big kiss!" The mouth closed; the mottled lips began their awful descent. "Piss off with your stinking bad breath!" screamed Victoria.

The woman went into a very pleasing frenzy. She leaped away from the pram as though it were electrified. Her jaw dropped, her eyes popped; she began to blubber. Then with a howl she fled into the house. Shortly afterwards out came Gran, looking much perplexed. "Quite ridiculous," she was saying . . . "only fifteen months old . . . absolute nonsense. Hello, Victoria darling."

"Goo goo gah!" said Victoria, waving her fist in the air and flashing a sidelong look of triumph at Madge, who was keeping her distance. "Gwan!" And Madge was sent on her way, with advice from Gran, who was having great trouble in choking back laughter, to take things a bit more easily. She must have been overdoing it lately. "Idiot woman!" said Gran to Victoria. "I always thought she was a bit unbalanced." And Victoria

95

chuckled happily.

The other low spots were concerned with the feeding and the plonking. Much of a baby's existence seemed to centre around the business of getting the right amount of food in and out of it at the right times; the key to being a successful baby was to co-operate fully with this process, at both ends. The eggies, which were scrambled, were tolerable, as was the wafer-thin bread and butter and honey, but sugared mashed banana was really a bit hard to take. Hamburger and chips, thought Victoria. Steak and chips, fish and chips, sausage and chips, chips and chips . . . "What a nice banana!" Gran said firmly, while with exceptional cruelty she fried a piece of fish for herself.

The potty was also a problem — there was a limit to what Victoria was prepared to do in it. This caused Gran much consternation, and produced mutterings of "such a regular little girl usually". But Victoria just sat there stubbornly, kicking her legs and saying "no no no"; eventually Gran gave in, said: "I suppose you know", and carried her back downstairs, after refastening the ever-present nappy.

Victoria was cuddled and bounced and told more than once that she was the most gorgeous darling in the whole world. "Goo," she said, for her experience of babies was practically non-existent, and she had no idea of how advanced in talking a child of her age should be. She had been told that she was an early talker, but this meant nothing without a standard against which to set it. It was better to err on the side of safety. Gran mustn't be alarmed.

Gran was lovely. She was so nice and smart and comfortable and sensible; taller than Victoria's mother, and stylishly slender. Her hair was soft and fair, greying slightly now, but she didn't look in the least bit old. Neither, happily, did she look young. The whole point of grandmothers was that they weren't young. Of course they had had a youth, way back in the Dark Ages, but it had no relevance to what they were now; it did not improve a grandmother, to imagine that she had once been a silly young girl herself. Victoria knew little of her grandmother's past. She had been born Dorothy Paige, just after the First World War; her husband had died of a heart attack in his forties. His wife, now

Dorothy Jacobs, had been left with a tidy sum in savings and insurance, and a near-teenage daughter, Patricia. It was the barest outline, but enough. The present grandmother was the one who mattered. Again, Victoria was grateful for the clock's demon accuracy in planting her slap in the middle of a time when her parents were away without her. It must be the middle, for there was no upheaval, no signs of recent arrival or imminent department.

She was put to bed ridiculously early, after causing much amusement by beginning to read a paperback novel (it was quite interesting, but Gran took it away), and more still by her attentive watching of a TV special about the Apollo space programme. "Look at you, for all the world as if you understood every word," said Gran fondly. "Buzaldrin," gurgled Victoria darkly. This was the sum total of her knowledge of the first moon landing, which seemed to be due to happen in a few weeks' time. She could never remember the name of the man who had been first out of the capsule — it was a dull name — but she knew Buzz Aldrin. "What was that?" asked Gran, and: "Goo," said Victoria.

And even after she had been tucked up in the cot, with a teddy bear and dozens of goodnight kisses, still she wasn't bored, although she knew it would be many hours before she slept. There was so much to think about. Already she had adjusted to the hugeness of the things around her, and now she looked at the gaily coloured mobiles that hung from the ceiling and rustled gently in the breeze from the window, at the cuddly toys, the squeaking jack-in-the-box, the little trolley full of plastic bricks, orange, yellow, green and blue, the baby-walker in the form of a fluffy white lamb, and she thought — what a wonderful room for a tot, how good of Gran to have all these nice things here for her small guest. And Victoria had done her bit. She had found her feet and toddled for all she was worth, she had played so cutely with all the toys — she had done very well, and they had both had a good day. Victoria felt rested, renewed, reinvigorated.

She looked at the clock, the cause of it all, sitting there sentry-like, measuring off the hours. If only she could get to it; if, *if* she were to rewind the hidden key, then what would happen? Would

97

she stay here? But she knew that even if it worked, it wouldn't be any good. This one day had been a delightful novelty — more could only lead to boredom and frustration. There could be no escape into the past. If she were to get away from 1983, there was only one way to go. Forwards. She must find the courage to set the clock for twenty-four, and to seek for happiness, however fleeting, in her own future.

TEN

Daniel got three A's. He rang with the news from a call box outside his school, which opened on the morning that the A Level results arrived.

"You could cut the atmosphere with a knife," he said. "There's about fourteen people sitting there waiting to go in and get their results, biting their fingers down to the bone. Someone said Paul Ruddock rushed out in tears just before I got there, and nobody's seen him since. Paul Ruddock! Crying!"

"These little setbacks are so good for the character," said Victoria. "What about you? I bet you've been practising a suitably modest expression for weeks. What did Esteemed Head Person have to say?"

"Potts? Oh, this gleam came into his eye when I went into the office, and he stood up, he actually got up, and said: "Ah, Priestley! Three of the best!" And I was just expecting old Wallis to appear with the cane, when I realized. And Potts shook my hand, and said: 'A superb result, Priestley! Jolly well done!' in his 'the British Empire has been saved again' voice. I don't really believe it yet. I mean, I know in my head that it's true, but I don't *believe* it."

"Mmm," said Victoria. She knew exactly what he meant. "Well — when will you be coming over? We have to celebrate."

"Victoria, I'm so very sorry, but I can't. Dad's arranged a family thing. His sister, my Auntie Joan's coming over with Uncle Ted, and his brother, my Uncle Malcolm, and we're

99

having this big dinner, Mum's going to be all day getting it ready . . ."

"Fantastic," said Victoria, bitterly.

"Look, I'm not going to enjoy it. I'm not looking forward to it at all. I'll have to put my best clothes on and be polite, and listen while they discuss me, and Auntie Joan will be patronizing Mum . . ."

"For God's sake, Daniel, then why do it? It's *your* day, it's *you* who got the A Levels, aren't you entitled to enjoy yourself? Tell him you've got a previous engagement."

"You know I can't do that. You're making it so difficult for me, Victoria, making me feel like a criminal. My father's so proud, he's so happy; I have to do this for him. It's only one evening, after all. And it might be good tactics, you know, to go along with him over this. He's been getting a bit nasty about you, lately — always complaining that I'm seeing you too much, that I don't seem to want to know my own family any more."

"*Stuff* Daniel's father," hissed Victoria, as the call ended in a flurry of pips and "sorry — no more change — ring you tomorrow".

"Why's that?" asked Mrs Hadley, who was sitting on the sofa, reading something called *The Use and Abuse of Preemptive Bids*. Victoria told her. "What a ridiculous man," said her mother, "shutting out everyone except family like this. Why not invite you too? Has he ever *met* you?"

"Certainly not. I'm Public Enemy Number One, the major threat to his family unity."

"He's a very near-sighted man if that's his attitude. He's going just the right way to have his children reject him. They'll grow up and he'll never see them again."

"Mm," said Victoria, unimpressed. Her mother was probably right, but it wasn't hard to be perceptive about other people. Seeing yourself as you really were; that was the tough one. She turned to go back to her room, but her mother said: "Oh, you may as well have some coffee now you're up" and went out to the kitchen. It was nine forty-five, and if it hadn't been for Daniel's call Victoria wouldn't have emerged from her bed for another hour and a half at least. But she was wide awake now — anger is

100

a very effective wakener. She might as well have the coffee. She sat down and pictured Mr Priestley being guillotined on West End Green, and his head bouncing off down the hill like a skittish cabbage, all the way to Kilburn. She pictured his eyes being pecked out by huge birds, blood dripping from their beaks. She didn't want Daniel tomorrow; she wanted him today. This was their summer. And what was she to do all day on her own? Lesley had a full-time holiday job in a clothes store — Victoria had scarcely seen her since the end of term. Holiday jobs were not Victoria's scene. Six or seven hours a day of standing behind a counter in a uniform flogging nylon undies to bad-tempered sweaty old women — what a way to spend a summer! Life wouldn't be worth living.

"You'll be getting your results soon," said her mother, trailing back with two mugs of coffee. Mrs Hadley drank coffee constantly. Her breath reeked of Brazilian Blend whenever Victoria was close enough to smell it, which was seldom. "It would be nice if you could get two A's as well — keep up a perfect record between you."

"Maths maybe," said Victoria; she suspected that in her preoccupied state her performance in the exam had not been her best, but surely she'd still get an A? "English never. You know I can't do English, so why do you expect anything?"

"You can do English," her mother said — "it's just more of an effort for you than Maths. You don't automatically come top. You're in the top stream for English, you've had some very good results. It's amazing, really, to think of you being old enough to do O Levels. It seems only yesterday that you were at Junior School. But you're growing up so quickly, these days. You've changed almost beyond recognition."

"I've *what?*" So fixed in Victoria's mind was the idea that her mother, tightly cocooned in her own misery, was scarcely aware of her daughter's existence, that this remark startled her.

"You've been so much nicer these past months. More sensible, mature . . . I was telling your grandmother. You're definitely becoming a nicer person."

Victoria blinked. Nicer? When she'd been going round with her head boiling over with hate and scorn and frustration, her mother thought she was nicer? Then she remembered the mock-suicide attempts, and all the other parent-angering stunts which she had planned with such care, her caustic sarcasm . . . how long ago, how futile, how infantile they now seemed. Nowadays she simply switched off, shut her parents out — and here was her mother interpreting it as the greatest breakthrough since oven chips.

"I'm sorry," she said. "It was quite unintentional."

"There you are," her mother said. "It took you ages to come out with that, and it didn't even sound convincing. Not long ago you'd have flashed it out like a bullet. You've changed. You *are* growing up. Fifteen and a half, sixteen next year . . . before long you'll be leaving home. It hardly seems possible."

"You're in favour of that, me leaving home, are you?"

"Yes, of course I am. When the time is right, when you're ready, then it's only natural. There's no point in clinging, trying to hang on." (Do you realize what you're saying, thought Victoria, do you *realize*?) "I was eighteen when I left. I think that's about right."

"Eighteen, were you?" Victoria drained her coffee. As always, it left a bitter aftertaste in her mouth — really she didn't know why she drank the stuff, especially first thing in the morning. Orange juice, which made your mouth feel *clean*, would be much better, but she never remembered until she'd finished the coffee. "1966. Where were you living then?"

"What, when I left home? I had a bedsit in Paddington . . ."

"No, I don't mean that — I mean before you left. Where were you and Gran?"

"Well — the house in Fulham, of course. She didn't move to Hambourne until 1970."

Fulham. So that's where it was. "I remember that house," said Victoria.

"Oh, you can't possibly remember it, you haven't seen it since you were two." She sounded unreasonably irritated. "It was a beastly little house."

"It was a lovely house. There was a big pink bath and a pink washbasin, and a great big kitchen with a boiler in the corner, and a little pantry on the left as you went out to the back garden, and outside there was an apple tree, and there were pot plants in all the windows. You're just saying it was beastly because you don't get on with Gran. She had the most gorgeous room for me when I was there; it had mobiles hanging from the ceiling, and . . ."

"That's enough!" Mrs Hadley's cheeks were growing pink, her mouth puckering. "No child of two remembers all that. You've got it from your grandmother. Haven't you? Why lie to me? What's your grandmother been telling you?"

"What's she got to tell me that you're so worried about? Are you afraid she'll tell me what Dad's been doing with all his money these last seven years?"

She had scored a direct hit. Her mother's cheeks faded rapidly from pink to white, that dead bloodless look that Victoria had seen once before. She didn't want to see any more. "Yes, I'm really growing up, aren't I?" she said, and went back to her room slamming the door like a punctuation mark: end of episode, chew it over well, Mother, before tuning in to next week's gripping instalment.

So there was a secret. There was a secret, and it seemed that Victoria's grandmother must know it too — everyone knew it except herself. She would find out. In the afternoon she telephoned Gran in Hambourne, but there was no answer. Well, that was to be expected — Gran, unlike some people, didn't waste precious summer days sitting around indoors. The secret must wait. What could it be, to produce such a violent reaction from her mother? A scandal — a gigantic skeleton hidden away in a cupboard — that was somehow costing her father a small fortune? But she had been over this so many times before. She could think of nothing new.

And there was nothing to do, which would have been all right if only there had been someone to do it with. No Daniel. No Lesley, no Sophie . . . there was still Alison, but even as she was dialling she remembered that the Bettses were sunning their pale, freckled selves in Ibiza all this week. Which left precisely nobody. Victoria wasn't going to stay here all day with that woebegone wretch. She would have to go out, but where? There was Oxford Street, but it was so hot to be looking round shops, and there'd be zillions of people there, and the tube would be like a micro-wave oven.

In the end she spent the afternoon in the cinema, which was at least air-conditioned. The film was the latest James Bond: entertaining junk. Whenever there was a horrible death, Victoria screwed her eyes up and pretended it was happening to Daniel's father. Never had she hated him so much. All these months he'd been playing a game with them. He'd allowed Daniel out on an invisible leash, and now he was making sure that she knew he was still the boss, that *he* would have Daniel on the important days, *he* would always come first, *he* would win in the end.

She mustn't let him win. And she had the secret weapon — the clock. If it could take her forward in time she would know who won. Say she set the clock for twenty-four. If it turned out that all was well, and Daniel with her, she could relax. If, though, he was still his father's puppet — at twenty-*seven*? — she would know that she must redouble her efforts right now. It must be an advantage to know.

But — oh Lord, the things that could go wrong! Daniel might be married to someone else, with three children . . . no. Not possible. Or was it? And there was worse, far worse. Suppose she were to wake up in 1990 or when ever, and discover that the lunatics had pressed the buttons and wiped out the world in a nuclear holocaust? How could she cope with that? The years that were left to her would be a living hell of hopelessness and fear, every day just waiting for the big bang. Or there were smaller, more personal tragedies. By 1990 Daniel might have been run over by a bus. She herself might be slowly dying of cancer — she might be already dead. Would she wake up sealed into the blackness of a coffin, with a body eaten away by worms, and die all over again from suffocation, if she didn't die of sheer terror first? *Coward*, she told herself — you're just trying to wriggle out of it. If Daniel had been run over by a bus, then she would find out the exact date of his death, and when that day came round she'd make sure he stayed indoors for every second of it. And cancer could be treated if it was caught early enough — with several years' notice you'd be OK, you'd just get yourself off to a clinic, double quick. So, in fact, what she was doing could not hurt, and might even turn out to be a life-saving measure. She

104

must get it into her head that nothing she might discover about the future was necessarily inevitable. She would have advance warning, and the chance to change it. (Except the nuclear war.) But probably the clock wouldn't work at all and she'd wake up to just another boring day in August 1983.

All the same, her hand was shaking as she prised open the hidden compartment, wound the key and set the hand on the little dial for about two-thirds of the way between twenty-three and twenty-four. All thoughts of her parents, of the secret, had disappeared from her mind. By the time she drifted off into an uneasy sleep, the setting of the clock had become less of an attempt to find out the future than a plain test of her own courage. She slept only fitfully, and dreamed of giant grey skulls in an empty grey sky, leering down at the wastes of a dead planet, its surface charred with rotting corpses.

ELEVEN

This time she felt the bed move. There was a creaking of springs and a pulling of sheets. Instantly she was fully awake, and realized, with awe, what must be happening. She had been disturbed by her transferral to 1991, that had been the *actual moment* — but then the bed moved again, in just the same way, and somebody made a 'grrummph' noise. The truth dawned: she was in a double bed, and someone was in it with her.

She lifted her head and looked anxiously at the hump on her left. Only the head was visible — a head of thick, dark hair. It looked as if it might be Daniel's — it had grown a lot if so, but it was the right colour. It must be Daniel! If not, then she was in bed with a complete stranger. It was the most embarrassing thing possible. If only he would turn round. She sat up carefully, not wanting to wake him, and shivered suddenly, for it was bitterly cold in the room. The window to her right was thickly frosted over. She leaned over hastily, her heart pounding, and looked at the face — and then her heart gave one last pound and sank, with a desolate thud. She had never seen this person before.

And then she blinked and looked more closely, for suddenly she wasn't so sure. It did look a bit like Daniel around the mouth. Really there was an uncanny resemblance — the face was much fuller, the skin coarser — but — oh thank you, Lord, even though you don't exist — it *was* Daniel. Daniel eight years on; no longer a boy, but a grown man. Now that she could see it, it seemed unbelievable that she could have made the mistake. And how much more handsome he had become! The too-gentle, almost feminine contours of his face had strengthened and hardened.

106

And yet, there was still something left of the old, wistful, sad-spaniel face, vulnerable now in sleep. He looked fantastic. If the room had not been so cold, Victoria would just have sat there, looking at him, until he woke. But she could endure it no longer, and huddled back down under the bedclothes, her arms already goose-pimpled, her breath visible steam. She was wearing a thick blue nightdress — not the most alluring of garments, but she could see the point of it. She was longing to know what she herself looked like — twenty-three years old — but that must wait.

So she had, after all the agonizing, come to no harm, and she had found out what she needed to know — the best possible news — within five minutes. If only she could switch back to 1983 right now! God alone knew what complications this day would hold for her. But — and suddenly she felt that her whole body had lighted up with happiness, and was glowing under the bedclothes — here she was, with Daniel. They had a flat together, just as she had hoped and planned, and now she'd be able to get through the next few years with her parents — she could get through anything, with this at the end to look forward to. Her courage had paid rich dividends.

The flat, or this bedroom at least, wasn't at all as she had imagined it. It was too cluttered for a start — and so cramped, and so cold! Was there no heating in this place? The double bed took up most of the room; there was a large, dark brown wooden wardrobe to the left, and next to it a cupboard, which didn't quite match. The furniture was ugly and battered — the whole room reeked of rented furnished accommodation. The walls and ceiling seemed to have been recently painted, but there was a large damp patch in the corner above the window. Outside it was still dark — a quarter to seven, the clock said. It was there by her side on a tiny wooden bedside table, squashed between a small lamp and a travelling alarm clock. Victoria recognized none of these things; nothing in the room except Daniel, and the clock. She was very glad of its sturdy familiarity, a lifeline back to her own time. Where was she? This might not be London at all, but some quite unknown town or city. Perhaps Cambridge. She guessed that this was a large, old house that had been divided up into a number of flats; the ceiling was disproportionately high, and the wall opposite her, behind which lay the rest of the flat, looked phoney and out of place — probably this had once been part of a much bigger room. A car drove past outside, then stopped, and Victoria recognized the expectant ticking over of an unpaid taxi. Somewhere, a baby was crying.

Daniel beside her grunted and twitched. Don't wake up yet, thought Victoria — I'm not ready. The problems of the day ahead were beginning to take on an alarming urgency. How would she manage if she was, say, at college? But she was twenty-three, and it was much more likely that she had a job. This would be far worse. Even assuming that she could find out where she worked, there was no way she could bluff her way through an entire day, whatever the job, however lowly. And in all modesty, and however raging the unemployment situation, it was most unlikely that good-looking, top-stream Victoria Hadley hadn't managed to find herself a fairly demanding form of employment. She would have to take the day off work. She screwed her face up in preparation for the blinding headache she would have when Daniel woke, and commanded her stomach to be nauseous. It was a bit queasy already. Daniel could ring them up for her. Everything would be taken care of.

The baby was still wailing; Victoria wished someone would shut it up. So inconsiderate, at this hour. And then Daniel heaved his body over and mumbled. "Victoria, for God's sake why don't you go and see to that child, before I strangle it." His voice, despite the tone, was improved by maturity, more delicious than ever. Victoria chuckled in sympathy — she knew how he felt, and she could strangle it herself, making that awful row ... but Daniel wasn't laughing, he was still looking at her, waiting, as if he really meant it — and then it sank in. Her baby — their baby — it was theirs! She was on her feet in seconds, reaching for the quilted dressing-gown that was hanging on a peg on the door. *Their* baby — they actually had a baby — who did it look like, what sex was it, what was it called ... a dozen questions tumbled through her head. And yet, it didn't seem real. She wasn't a mother; she hadn't had a baby.

The door led out into a tiny hallway. There was a stand, smothered with coats and boots and shoes, and three other doors, one to the left, one to the right, one straight ahead. There was an ill-fitting piece of grubby-looking grey carpet on the floor, and a light bulb hung down from the ceiling on a frayed-looking piece of flex. There was no shade on it, and it looked rather dangerous. Victoria took all this in in a second. The door to the right was open, and it was from there that the crying came. My baby? she thought, and in a dream she went in.

At first she thought she had stepped into a cupboard by mistake, so small was the room, but then, from the dim light in the hall, she was able to make out the shape of a bed, tight against the left-hand wall. Not one bed. Bunk beds. There were *two* children here. It all began to seem too much. One child, yes, but two was an unnecessary complication — she didn't know where to look first — and all of a sudden she felt the stirrings of panic, felt a powerful impulse to turn and run, to run out of the flat and away from this family, these unknown people cooped up in this sardine tin of a flat, people of whom she knew nothing. She couldn't cope with all this.

But then the small body in the lower bunk resumed its grizzling cries, and Victoria pulled herself together sharply. *Not* strangers — Daniel, you fool, Daniel and his children — your children. Hesitantly, nervously, she perched on the edge of the bed, hunched over to avoid banging her head on the one above, and picked up the baby, praying that she was doing it right. It wasn't really a baby — it was a child of two or three, a miserable damp-faced child. Victoria hadn't been able to determine the sex of the one above, but this one was a girl; a little girl who knew her and was clinging to her now as if this had been all she wanted — the presence of her mother.

But I don't know you, thought Victoria. I may have given birth to you, though I can't imagine it, I can't believe it just now, but I simply know nothing about you, not even your name. The child gave a few last, half-hearted, soggy gulps and buried its head contentedly into Victoria's dressing-gown. Victoria wondered if she should be feeling some powerful emotion, a torrent of maternal love surging through her. She felt nothing but confusion.

The bulge in the mattress above shifted itself with a tiny sleepy noise, and the little girl suddenly pulled away from Victoria, sensing something wrong, displeased and puzzled by the unfamiliar stiffness and tension of her mother's body. "Oh please don't start crying again," said Victoria. She could see the child's face now. She had short, fair hair; her face was round and flattish, smudgy now with tears; her eyes were watery blue. She looks like me, thought Victoria, dazed, except that her ears stick out just like Daniel's. She remembered a game from the first or second year at St. Catherine's — a group of girls in her form, proudly announcing the number of children they intended to have, and their names. "I'm going to have two girls and two boys, called blah, blah, blah and blah . . ." Victoria had treated all this with scorn. She could remember saying cruelly to Phil Barton: "and what if you're *sterile*?" But in private she had played the game herself, choosing names only, for she hadn't been sure that she wanted the actual children to go with them. Ever since then she had periodically updated the list, and currently her favourite girls' names were Rebecca, Sarah, Emma, Alexandra. This child looked like an Emma. Did I call you Emma? she wondered silently. But it would be a stupid thing to risk frightening the child by calling her by a strange name. She could so easily be Sarah.

"Why don't you go back to sleep for a little while," she said in a low voice — "back under the bedclothes in the warm." Emma/Sarah looked up at her, her lower lip jutting out, and then rolled away without a word. I wonder what's going on in that head of yours, thought Victoria, feeling oddly rejected. She padded back out to the hall, hugging the dressing-gown closely to her, and opened the door opposite. This led to the rest of the flat — a room maybe half as big again as the first bedroom. Victoria stood still, appalled. Was this all? Kitchen and living-room, crammed into a space not big enough for either . . . where was the bathroom? She went back to the front door, and cautiously turned the Yale lock. Outside was a large landing, with stairs going up, stairs going down and two other front doors, numbered eight and nine, Victoria turned her head; their own was number seven. Opposite, a door was open, and Victoria could see the end of a bath in the room behind it. A communal bathroom. How absolutely nauseating. Sharing a bathroom, the most personal of rooms, with total strangers . . . were they so poor, then, that they had to live in this dump? If they were so hard up then why have children?

She went back inside, found some matches and lit the gas fire. How could people live without central heating in winter? Then an alarm went off, and there began what was to be one of the most exhausting hours of her life. Daniel stumbled out, tousled in his pyjamas, and said: "Kids not up yet?" and Victoria realized, to her utter horror, that she would have to get the children out of bed, take them to the bathroom, dress them, cook breakfast for four people . . . none of them things she had ever done before.

The children growled and whined, and of course there was someone else in the bathroom and they had to wait, and Emma/Sarah started snivelling again. "*Stop* that," snarled Victoria, hating her, for she was longing to talk to Daniel, to fulfil her dream of getting up with him, sitting with him at breakfast in leisurely fashion, sipping coffee and chattering about the day ahead — and there was no time, these bloody brats were demanding all her attention. There was a chest, crammed with clothes, squashed into their cupboard-room. Victoria took out the nearest things to hand and began, awkwardly, to dress them. The other one was a boy — how tidy, one of each — and older; thank God, five years old or thereabouts. With any luck he'd be at school all day; she didn't know yet exactly what the date was, but it couldn't be Christmas, or there would be decorations up. The boy seemed capable of dressing himself, so Victoria gave her full attention to manoeuvring the girl's mutinously unhelpful body into a red jumper and blue corduroys, tiny doll-sized garments.

So much, then, for her wonderful job! I must be a very different person, eight years on, thought Victoria, dragging a comb through Emma/Sarah's hair, while the boy tugged at her sleeve, whimpering something about socks — I must be different if this is what I do. I must really *love* these kids; nobody could bear it otherwise. It was hard to believe. Their very presence made her uncomfortable. She didn't know how to talk to them — she didn't know *anything* about small children. And they were intruding.

"Could you get on with the breakfast, do you think?" asked

Daniel, who had dressed and shaved, and was now sitting at the shabby drop-leaf table in the living-room. You might give me a hand, Victoria thought, steering the children, dressed, and, to the best of her ability, washed, into the room. But she just said: "What do you want?", hoping against hope that he wouldn't say "the usual, of course."

"Bacon and eggs," Daniel said abruptly. He hadn't hugged her, he'd hardly spoken to her, he hadn't come *near* her. Had they quarrelled the night before? There was an ancient gas cooker in the kitchen half of the room, and next to it squatted a small gas fridge. Victoria managed to negotiate bacon and eggs for two successfully; she had wondered if the children were supposed to have the same, but the boy solved the problem by shouting out: "I want Wheaty Bits today!" This sounded like a cereal; Victoria spent five minutes searching through cupboards before it dawned on her that he meant Weetabix. "What's the matter with you today?" said Daniel. "You know he calls them Wheaty Bits. Try not to burn the bacon next time, would you? What was the matter with Stella?"

Stella? A child of hers called *Stella?* How could it be? There are names you simply know you will never like, not in eight years' time or eighty, and for Victoria Stella was one of them. For crying out loud, what had they named the boy? Walter? Horace?

She preferred the boy, so far. He was a handsome little thing, with Daniel's dark hair and huge dark eyes, and being older than Stella he could do more for himself. She would prefer him still more when he'd gone to school, which it was apparent from his chatter — "Miss *Cooper* takes the *register!*" he was about to do. Victoria was rather grateful for his prattling, because nobody else was saying anything at all. She would have liked him to be called Toby, Ben or Nicholas, but somehow after Stella she feared the worst.

And now it was Victoria who felt like the intruder — like a guest paying a courtesy visit to seldom-seen relations. The lady of the house had been taken ill, and Victoria was standing in for her. Even Daniel was a stranger. Somehow he had discarded his old vulnerable look and acquired nasty prickles; he was giving off very strong "don't touch me" vibrations. "Don't forget to pick up my trousers from the cleaners," he said, and that was all. This is a play, thought Victoria; Daniel is acting, the children are someone else's. It can't be for real. "Eat your breakfast, Stella," said Daniel. "I want you to finish every mouthful."

"Don't like," said Stella. It was the first time she had spoken.

"Why on earth have you given her Weetabix?" said Daniel. "You know she won't eat anything but Ready Brek."

"Oh — I'll give her some Ready Brek in a while," said Victoria. "I wasn't thinking. I'm tired." This was the truth. She could very easily have gone back to bed and slept for another five hours. It was, in a way, a relief when Daniel finished his breakfast, got up from the table and went out — presumably to work. She was making the inevitable mistakes, and his presence was an enormous strain. Dismally she surveyed the pile of greasy washing-up, and began reluctantly to stack it in the orange plastic bowl which sat inside the stained, enamel sink. She'd do it later. Daniel kissed her cheek on his way out, but with about as much feeling as if he were kissing the door. It felt more like a blow.

"Time for *school*," the boy said, bouncing about with what Victoria guessed to be the excitement of one who has just started this September, and to whom it is all still a glorious adventure. "We'll be *late*, Mummy. Miss Cooper will be calling the *register*. Please, hurry, Mummy," he wailed, in an agony of frustration.

"All right, all right." So she had to take him, and Stella couldn't be left on her own, so she'd have to come too. Victoria went into her bedroom, saw a dress flung over a small chair by the door, and wriggled into it at speed. It was the most boring drab brown thing — she didn't think much of the future Victoria's taste in clothes, if this was a typical example. I've seen sacks I'd rather wear, she thought, stuffing Stella's unyielding arms into the little red coat which hung on the stand in the hall. There were also two little woolly scarves, four woolly mittens and four miniature blue wellington boots. Clearly the children must be well wrapped. But this took time, especially with Victoria's clumsy, unaccustomed fingers doing the wrapping, and the boy howled anew. "I think I shall go mad if we don't go soon," he said with a sob. "*Coming*," said Victoria.

113

A bunch of keys hung on a nail by the door; surely these must include the keys to the house and to the flat. She put them into her coat pocket — a heavy grey coat, little better than the dress. "Now — have you got everything?" she said to the boy, and hustled them out and down the stairs, to another landing, this one with a coin-box phone and doors numbered four, five and six, and then down more stairs to the hall. There was another phone here, and, by the wall, a pile of dog mess, spiralling up into a little point like ice-cream in a cone. "Watch out for that," said Victoria, wrinkling her nose. There was also a long table, with the morning's post laid out on it — nothing for Priestley, but perhaps Daniel had taken it with him. Was she really Mrs Priestley now? It sounded very old and matronly. It sounded like somebody else.

There was a row of bells outside the front door; a little card saying "Priestley" was slotted in beside number seven. Their neighbours in eight and nine, according to the cards, were O'Connor and Aziz. Seven stone steps led down to the pavement. "Now," said Victoria to the boy, "this morning we're going to play a special game. You be me and I'll be you. You're Mummy, and you're taking me to school on my very first day."

"Oh yes!" squeaked the boy, looking up at her in rapture. "I'm Mummy, and you must hurry along to school now, Robert, or you'll be late." Robert, thought Victoria, and sighed. "This way, Robert; this is the way. Miss Cooper will be taking the register, and when she says your name you say yes miss. Now we're going to cross over the road. Take your sister's hand, Robert; you know she's smaller than you are. Oh yes, Robert, you must always take care of your sister."

"No!" yelped Stella. "Hold *Robert*'s hand."

"Be quiet — I *am* Robert," said Victoria, who suspected that Stella was going to be big trouble, and should be put in her place at the earliest opportunity. They crossed the road, turned left into a main road, over a crossroads, over the road again and there was the school, the shrieking children, and hordes of mothers depositing them. "Now, be a good boy, Robert!" said Robert, triumphantly.

"What time will you come and collect me, Mummy?" asked Victoria, and Robert said sternly:

"I'll be here at half past three, I won't be late like some of the mothers, I'll be the *first one here*" — a hint if ever she heard one. She waved at him as he scampered off across the playground — not a bad kid, and he couldn't help being called Robert. Victoria, clearly, had had no say in the naming of the children at all. Why not? Had they tossed a coin for it? She turned, thoughtfully, and set off back for the flat, Stella scuttling along furiously by her side, blinking in the sharp wind, saying nothing.

Although she couldn't quite place it, this area was not totally unfamiliar to Victoria. Certainly they were in London — "City of Westminster" was written on all the street signs, and red buses trundled by on their way to Oxford Circus, Marble Arch and Tottenham Court Road. London, but where? Surely she had seen this main road before. They turned into the street where they lived, alliteratively named Ackerson Avenue. There might be an A to Z amongst the jumble of books in the bedroom and living-room, and she could look it up.

Not even the most devious and euphemistic of estate agents could possibly have described Ackerson Avenue as a desirable area. It had the uncared-for, uncared-about look of a bedsitter world with a transient population. Ancient, peeling, decaying houses towered up to the sky on either side, several of them derelict and abandoned, the glassless windows like giant empty eye-sockets. There were small bits of garden in front of some of the houses at the main road end, but no flowers grew in Ackerson Avenue. The gardens were rubbish tips. In one of them sat an old refrigerator, surrounded by broken glass; in a second, two faded yellow doors, and in a third — Victoria blinked — a bath.

There was nothing around her to show that eight years had passed. On the surface, London looked much the same as ever. Though what did she expect? That the Government would in 1988 have ordered all the roads to be painted purple, and the pavements pink? A car freak would have been aware of dozens of new models, but Victoria was not interested in cars. There was nothing at all remarkable about the clothes and hairstyles of the people she had seen. It was all rather comforting. I must buy a paper, she thought; she had almost reached the newsagent and general store at the far end of Ackerson Avenue, Stella stumping along a pace behind her, before she realized that she had no money. Back they went; the third key she tried opened the front door, the second key opened the door to the flat, and as they crossed the threshold she crumpled with relief. Surely the worst was over. There was nobody to see her now — Stella didn't count — and she could do as she liked.

And really, she thought, patiently unwrapping Stella, she had done stupendously well so far. She had woken in a place and a situation about which she knew nothing, and — although it hadn't felt that way at the time — she had coped magnificently. She'd done the breakfast and got the children up, and Robert off to school, and nobody had suspected a thing. Except Stella. Stella knew quite well that this was a stranger disguised as her mother. Well, Stella would have to live with that for a day. It wouldn't do her any permanent damage. Victoria knew the workings of her clock well enough by now to be sure of that. This day would never really happen.

She looked with great loathing at the pile of plates in the sink, glistening with fat, and, reluctantly, set about washing them. Best to get it out of the way. Then she made Stella some Ready Brek, and went out to the newsagents, leaving her to eat it. She should be safe enough. She couldn't light the oven, and it was unlikely that she would manage to incinerate herself on the gas fire within five minutes, though there was always hope.

When Victoria got back, Stella was still at the table apparently quite unconcerned at having been left alone, spooning away the Ready Brek with an inscrutable expression. Victoria tossed the paper on to a chair, and went into the bedroom to look closely at herself in the mirror. She'd been dying to do this ever since she woke, but there hadn't been any time. It was a grotty little mirror, only about twenty inches by twelve, but the flat held nothing better.

She hardly knew herself. It was most unnerving, almost frightening, to look into a mirror and see a stranger. She was sure she looked older than twenty-three.

Her skin had an unhealthy, almost greyish pallor; her eyes

116

were sunk into dark rings, the giant panda effect which she'd so often noticed on her mother. She looked tired, and unwell. Her face, like Daniel's, was fuller and heavier; so, she had been aware all day, was her body. Presumably you couldn't expect to have two children and still look like a fragile doll, and in fact the extra weight improved her figure, or what she could see of it. But all in all she found her reflection disturbing. There was something about it, the washed-out face in particular, which reminded her — and this was painful to admit — of her mother. She badly needed make-up, but all she could find was some ghastly face power and one insipid pink lipstick. No mascara, no eye-shadow, no nail varnish — Victoria thought with longing of the splendid array of cosmetics which she owned, back in 1983. She could transform herself, if she had them here now. But even the lipstick was an improvement, bringing a faint touch of life to that dead face.

And now, she really must change out of this revolting dress into something pretty. She dragged open the stiff wardrobe door. On the right were jackets, men's trousers and shirts, all neatly arranged on hangers, and on the left, what must be her clothes. They must be hers, for there were no other adult females living here. And they were appallingly dull. Respectable, plain, high-necked long-sleeved dresses, stark grey skirts, off-white blouses — Victoria reeled backwards in disappointment. There wasn't a single garment that was any fun. She thought of the lovely clothes she'd planned to buy when she had a job and lots of money. She might as well keep the brown dress on — there was certainly nothing better, and at least it was comfortable for knocking around the flat. Had she really developed such sober tastes? She doubted it. Something was beginning to click in the back of her mind. These clothes, like the children's names, had been chosen by someone else. And the list of candidates was extremely limited.

When she went back to the living-room Stella had eaten the Ready Brek. She had also eaten the newspaper, or was in the process of doing so. Every single page had been shredded into easily digestible-sized pieces, and even as Victoria rushed to grab them a large chunk of the sports section disappeared into Stella's mouth. "For God's sake!" shouted Victoria, as Stella defiantly chewed her way through Aston Villa's midweek triumph over Manchester United. "Are you out of your mind?" Stella expressed no opinion on this, nor did she make any attempt to retain the remainder of the paper. Victoria hurled it all into the pedal bin in a fury. Would it harm her? Was newsprint poisonous? Probably not. She was bloody well going to chance it. Time enough to panic when Stella started vomiting, which the little brat would probably manage to do out of spite. "Maniac!" she yelled. There was no response. There was something about Stella that reminded Victoria of a TV programme she'd seen about autistic children — blondly beautiful, withdrawn, uncommunicative, unreachable, locked away in their own impenetrable world. Except that Stella was very much on the ball; of that Victoria was sure. "All right —" she said venomously — "if I have to watch you every moment then I'll *watch* you. Now come along in here with me." She hauled Stella into the bedroom, and left her spluttering with rage on the floor.

Now. Somewhere in this flat, and almost certainly in this room, there must be papers; documents which would cast some light on the events of the past eight years, which would help her to trace the path that had brought them to this point, to this undersized dump in Paddington. She hadn't been able to find an A to Z, but she'd seen the *Paddington Mercury*, on sale in the newsagents. Paddington . . . "I lived in a bedsit in Paddington," her mother had said. With a growing, uneasy sense of patterns repeating themselves, she set about her search.

Because she didn't immediately think to look under the bed, it took fully twenty minutes before she struck gold. Two suitcases, one blue, one brown. This just had to be it. The blue case had a thick film of dust right across it, and contained stacks of books, files and notes, all of them Daniel's from his university years, as was obvious from the scientific nature of the material, and its great complexity. Victoria dug right down to the bottom, but there was nothing else. She snapped the case shut, shoved it back under the bed in a nose-pricking dusty cloud, and reached for the second case. There was very little dust on this one; it had been used more frequently, more recently.

This was the one. There were two large photograph albums, and a buff-coloured folder with "Documents and Certificates" neatly printed on it in Daniel's writing. She grabbed it and surveyed the riches within. Birth certificates, National Health cards, passports, the lot — plus a pile of less interesting, more impersonal things: TV licence, premium bonds, insurance documents, business letters. And a certificate of marriage. Victoria picked this up, again expecting a surge of emotion, or *something* — but it was just a piece of paper, and although it certainly said, "Victoria Louise Hadley", it seemed quite unrelated to herself. So they were married; they had married in October 1985, at Marylebone Registry Office. Good — no church nonsense, not that she would ever have agreed to it, massive hypocrisy, not to mention the waste of money. 1985. She had been just seventeen, so it looked as if she'd never finished school, never done her A Levels after all. And Daniel — he would have been twenty. In October 1985 he *should* have started his final year at Cambridge. What had happened to that? Why had they married at a time that was so obviously twelve months too early? She had a nasty feeling that she knew. Patterns, repeating themselves . . .

The first of the birth certificates was her own, which she'd seen many times before, and under it was Daniel's, recording the birth of Daniel John, to Robert John Priestley and Mary Stella Priestley, formerly Davis, on April 30th, 1965. It also confirmed that Daniel was a boy, which was good to know. Then came the birth certificates of the two children, both born at St. Mary's Hospital, Paddington. On September 3rd 1988, Stella Victoria Mary, and on March 10th 1986, Robert Daniel John. Apart from that token Victoria, the children had been solidly named after the Priestleys. How could she have allowed her son to be named after Daniel's father? Had she been in a coma at the time? She looked again at the date: March the tenth. That was her own birthday. It was also just five months after their marriage.

"Well, Stella," she said, "I think we've found out why your Dad and I got married in such a hurry. Two and two, Stella, you will generally discover, make four." Stella was methodically chewing her way through a card with four large black buttons on it. Victoria removed the card. Well. They had been stupid, hadn't they? They had got married for the benefit of the imminent, and by that time probably noticeable, Robert. And thereby they had more than likely cut off Daniel's education in its prime, for he would have had to work to support them — and with unemployment the way it was headed in 1983 he'd have had to take anything he could get, and supporting three, and later four, people on that one salary could not have been easy. And that was why they were where they were now. And she, Victoria, had self-destructed into a housewife, a full-time mother-drudge — surely the thing in all the world that she was least suited for. Daniel's father had, without any doubt, thrown him out and done the full "never darken my door again" scenario. Not an auspicious start. Nothing romantic about it at all — just very stupid. Well — now she knew. She was forewarned. She would see that it didn't happen. She would finish school, and Daniel would finish Cambridge, and they would both get good jobs, and *then* they would get together, just the two of them, no tiny feet pattering, no tiny mouths eating cardboard . . . she lunged at Stella, who had found another card, this one containing six poppers. No, none of this. She had been given a way out.

She leafed through the rest of the papers. The business letters turned out to be carbons of Daniel's job applications. There were a dozen or more, addressed to firms of which Victoria had never heard, excepting British Telecom, and to each one was tidily stapled a brief letter of rejection. What very odd things to keep. Still, it did confirm her earlier suspicions; work had not been easy to come by. There were also a couple of vaccination certificates for a cat called Snowy. Victoria wondered what ill fate had befallen Snowy. Probably splat under a car, unless Stella had eaten him at a time of paper shortage.

The photographs in the albums were nearly all of Daniel's family. He must have sneaked them out with him when he left home for the last time. Victoria flipped through with interest; there was Mr Priestley, great patriarch of renown, older and balder than she'd pictured him; Mrs Priestley, whom she'd seen at various school functions, a little shadow of a woman; Daniel and Sophie at different ages and sizes, Daniel looking very enigmatic from an early age, his face giving nothing away. A neat little caption was written under each picture: "Skegness, summer '72" . . . "in the garden, Joan's and Ted's visit, Easter '76". The Priestley family history. The visible proof of the great patriarch's diligence. He must have had kittens when he found they'd gone. She searched for wedding photos, but there weren't any.

Time had flown past — she glanced up at the clock as she put everything back, and, incredibly, it was a quarter to one. She took Stella back into the kitchen and began to bang around with the grill pan. They would have cheese on toast, and Stella would like it or do without. But the grill refused to light, and the fire had gone out. Victoria shivered suddenly. What was wrong? Oh — *gas*. Where was the meter — oh, yes, under the sink. The slot was far too small — only big enough for a 5p piece, which was ridiculous — and then she remembered the one pound coin, which had been issued to rapturous indifference just a few months before, from her point of view. Luckily there were a couple in the purse she'd taken when she went to buy the newspaper.

They ate in uncompanionable silence, and then Victoria decided that Stella should have a nap. Stella didn't altogether agree with this, but after ten ear-splitting minutes her roars subsided into what Victoria hoped would be a long deep sleep — like twelve hours, for instance. Victoria was very tired herself, mentally as well as physically. She desperately needed to rest — some time to herself to get things straight, to absorb everything that had happened and that she had learned. There were two dark green armchairs in the living-room; she flopped down in the nearer of the two, curled up until she was quite comfortable, and began to think.

TWELVE

It was half past one. Two more hours and she could fetch Robert; after that another, say, seven hours, and she could go to bed — oh, she'd be very tired tonight. And then it would be over. Just nine more hours to get through. But at some point Daniel would be coming home, and this she was dreading. How could she fool him for an entire evening? She tried not to think of it. He'd been in a bad temper earlier, but then so were millions of other people, just after they'd got up. Maybe he'd come back more cheerful — but also more wide-awake, more alert, more likely to pounce on her smallest mistake. If the worst came to the worst and she knew she couldn't carry it off, she'd just have to plead a blinding headache and go to bed at seven. She so wished it were all over.

In many ways, she had to admit, she'd been lucky. She'd been able to find everything she needed with no trouble; nothing had been expected of her that she couldn't do — driving a car, for instance. Nobody had come knocking at the door, nobody had stopped to speak to her in the street. Perhaps the future Victoria had few friends and a lonely life. She had been trying to piece this person, the future Victoria, together, to form an Identikit picture from the scraps of evidence around her. It was impossible. She was a non-smoker (no ashtrays, no cigarettes) — a very dull dresser, a shunner of artificial aids to beauty. She seemed to like wine — there were a couple of bottles of Chianti in the corner. And that was it. There was no shred of her personality anywhere; it was as if the future Victoria walked around with an eraser, rubbing herself out before she had time to make an impression.

There were no clues to her hobbies, pastimes or interests — if she had any. If she had time, with two small children to look after. It was all so very different from the person Victoria was now, and from what she had expected to become. What had happened to her? Victoria remembered how she'd discovered Daniel beside her, first thing that morning, and thought: bliss, heaven, beam me up Scotty, I've found out all I need to know. Kiddo, you're learning fast.

She no longer cared about the destruction of her newspaper. She could have switched on the radio or the television, but she felt no desire to do either. The world outside would be too much to handle. She didn't want to know, didn't need to know; she would find out all that had happened gradually, as she lived through the eight years. That was the best way. Her visit to 1991 was concerned solely with her personal future. Suddenly she thought of her parents, and wondered what they had made of all this. They wouldn't have cared what she did; certainly they wouldn't have thrown her out for getting herself pregnant at seventeen. That wasn't their style. More like:

"Victoria's having a baby, Simon. She's getting married on Saturday."

"Oh, I see, Pat. So my daughter's proven fertility is supposed to account for the fact that you failed even to make a slam *try* holding ten points when I'd opened two no trumps. Six spades was stone cold on any lead . . ." If, that is, they were still together. How long had that shambles dragged on? Victoria got up, took some coins from the purse, went down to the phone on the floor below, and dialled their number. Pip pip pip pip clunk. "Hello?" said a female voice.

"Hello? Is that . . . is Mrs Hadley there?"

"I'm sorry, you must have the wrong number. There's noboby here of that name."

"Sorry to bother you," Victoria said, deflated, and trailed back up to the flat. It told her nothing, either way. She couldn't understand why she felt so disappointed. She had really *wanted* the voice that answered to be her mother's. She peeked in at Stella, who was breathing heavily in her sleep, and didn't stir. Then she returned to the armchair and fell asleep herself.

She was woken by a short, sharp noise, and sat up in alarm. How long had she slept? What time was it? The noise came again. *Blast* it. Somebody knocking at the door. She longed to ignore it, but she couldn't, it might be important, it might be *Daniel* . . .

"Come to empty your meter, love," said the man. "Hope I didn't disturb you. You look as if you've just woken up."

"I have," said Victoria. "It doesn't matter. What time is it?"

"'Bout ten past three," said the man, and went about his business, Victoria keeping a close eye on him — not that there was much here worth stealing. Then Stella had to be woken, and there was all that hassle with coats and mittens again, for it was time to fetch Robert.

They must have been early, for there were only a very few mothers waiting, and the children were just beginning to trickle out. The mother next to Victoria was wearing one of the most outrageous garments she had ever seen: a giant poncho, crocheted in granny squares of livid pink red and orange glitter nylon. Victoria blinked. And there was Robert, hurtling across the playground with another small boy, deliriously excited to see her. "Oh, she's here!" he shrieked. "Look, she's here already!" The nearby mothers looked sidelong at Victoria with thinly veiled amusement. Victoria scowled. The little boy with Robert was very eyecatching; he had tight little red lips, brilliant red cheeks, a runny nose, and was wearing a very nasty coat of yellow plastic. He looked exactly like a Grisholm. And somehow Victoria wasn't at all surprised when he was claimed, with a cuff on the ear and a "wipe your nose, can't you?" by the mother in the poncho. *Sharon* — no, too young to be Sharon. It wasn't Cherry . . . by God, it was Demelza. Demelza Grisholm! With a son of five, and she couldn't be more than twenty herself. "What you staring at?" said Demelza, with native Grisholm charm.

"I think I used to be at school with your sister," said Victoria.

"Which one? I got four of them."

"Cherry — and Sharon."

"That's nice for you," said Demelza, and turned to go, grabbing the boy by the collar.

"What are they doing now?" asked Victoria, suddenly curious.

"Doing? How should I know? Cherry ran off when I was twelve, nobody's heard of her since. Sharon met a bloke and went up north after she come out of Borstal. How should I know what they're doing? Come *on*, will you, Conan?"

"Conan's mummy's very pretty, isn't she?" said Robert, on the way home.

"You've got very dubious tastes for one so young," said Victoria, and then. "What's—er—Conan's surname, Robert?"

"Grisholm," said Robert, and Victoria nodded; so Demelza hadn't troubled herself with a husband. Demelza. The last time Victoria had seen her, just a few months ago, she'd been five years old. Now she was twenty. It was disorientating, even for such a seasoned time traveller as Victoria. And she found it somehow depressing that not only should her son be attending the same school as Demelza's, but that they should be pals. It was, she felt, a pointed comment on their social status.

Robert really was a little life-saver. As soon as they got back he went straight over to the television, switched it on, changed the channel and said: "Come on, Stella; it's time for our programme now." And that was the two of them taken care of. They watched quite indiscriminately, gazing as if hypnotized at whatever came on. Victoria made marmite sandwiches, cake and orange squash for them, and left them to it. She could afford to relax for a while now; to sit quietly and gather her strength for when Daniel came home.

Robert really was rather gorgeous. The way he wrinkled his nose and cocked his head to the left, just like Daniel . . . they must have wanted him so much, for they had sacrificed a great deal for him. She'd have been able to get an abortion with no trouble at all, but no, they'd gone ahead and had him. It was rather horrible, she thought with a sudden pang, the first really powerful emotion she'd felt all through that strange day, that she was going to murder him. No, that was too strong. She was going to prevent him. She had already decided that neither child could possibly be allowed to exist. Logically, it wasn't as bad as abortion, because she was going to prevent him altogether — but of course it was really ten million times worse, because she had seen him, known him, however briefly, as an active, happy little boy. Oh — but she couldn't have children so young, it was all wrong for her, this life wouldn't be any good for any of them . . . it was a moral dilemma of nightmarish proportions. If only Robert were as unlovable as Stella, if only she didn't *care*. But surely in a few months' time the memory of Robert would have faded. She must try to wipe him from her mind. It was the only way.

Daniel came home at six, just as the regional news programme was starting. His temper appeared little improved. "Had a good day?" Victoria asked timidly, and Daniel exploded.

"A good day? What's that supposed to mean? Have I had one single good day in the entire two and a half years that I've worked for Messrs. the Almighty Bishop and Heller?" Clearly, as opening remarks go, Victoria's had been a second *Titanic*. "I've had a stinking, lousy day, just like all the others. That pompous strutting little twit of a Jones . . . if you had the *imagination* to realize what it's like, day in, day out, taking orders from a bloke with less than a *tenth* of your brain, cleaning up after him, saying yes sir, no sir, you're right sir, just because he's got a bloody piece of paper that you haven't . . . oh God, how I wish I'd got that degree! I'd be stamping on his face now." He was pacing around the room, his face black thunder. "It's so frustrating . . . oh, but we've been through all this before — what's the point?" Victoria said nothing, for fear of saying something wrong. "Oh well," said Daniel, and sat down. To Victoria's surprise, he scooped Stella up into his lap, and bounced her on his knee. Stella cooed with delight. "And how's my little lady?" said Daniel, tickling her.

"Daddy tickle!" squealed Stella, with a malevolent glance at Victoria. Well. What a very touching scene.

"Mum rang me at work," said Daniel.

"Oh yes?" Victoria said carefully. This was very unexpected.

"Dad's working late tomorrow, so she's coming round to see the kids. She'll be here about four. Make sure you've got something nice to give her, will you, cake or something. She's bringing her Christmas presents, in case she doesn't get another chance."

"Yes," said Victoria, and understood. Mrs Priestley had struck out with a little secret gesture of defiance. She had kept in touch with Daniel, and sneaked over to see her grandchildren whenever the ogre was out of the way. Happy families.

"What time will the chops be ready?" asked Daniel.

"Chops?"

"I thought you said that you were getting chops for dinner tonight."

"No . . . I didn't get chops."

"Well, what is it then?"

"I . . . well . . . I didn't get anything special. What would you like?"

"What do you mean, what would I like? Victoria, did you get something for dinner or didn't you? What's the matter with you? Isn't there something cooking?"

"Not actually, not at the moment . . ."

"Oh, I don't *believe* this." He lifted Stella to the floor. "Look, Victoria, I hope I'm not being unreasonable, but I've just got in after a long, tiring, frustrating day's work, and you're playing some game with me . . . I mean, what's going on here? Have you got my dinner on or not?"

"Daniel, wait, listen," Victoria said desperately. Why, oh why hadn't she thought of an evening meal? "I haven't been well today. I think I've got a virus . . ."

"Oh, you've got a *virus*, I see, so you stop everything; well, you're lucky to have that luxury. When I felt so terrible last month, did I take a single day off work? No, I didn't. I staggered in and did my job, because if I don't, where's the money going to come from? But you, do you do your bit? No. You've got a *virus* . . ."

This was turning into a nightmare. "Stop it, Daniel, please don't go on so. I'm very sorry — what more can I say? I was just feeling so rotten, and I didn't think you'd mind . . ."

There was a moment's silence. "Oh well," said Daniel, "the doctor's surgery's open till seven. If you're really ill you'd better go along and see her — but who's going to put the children to bed? Have *they* had something to eat?"

"Oh yes," said Victoria. "It's all right, I'll see to the kids. If I still feel like this tomorrow I can go to the morning surgery. It might just turn out to be a twenty-four-hour thing. There is one going around." There always was, at this time of year.

"You don't look that bad," said Daniel, scrutinizing her. "You don't sound as if you've got a cold."

"No — it's a head thing," said Victoria, vaguely. She ought to have stuck to a headache, but a virus sounded so much worse.

"You make sure you go tomorrow. And ask her to take a blood sample or something. You might be anaemic."

"Yes, Daniel," said Victoria. "Come along, Robert, Stella, time for bed." She steered the children firmly into their bedroom, ignoring Robert's howls of protest. Escape.

"It's so *early*," wailed Robert.

"Not at all," said Victoria. The sooner the children were packed away, the sooner she could go to bed herself. She simply couldn't cope wtih Daniel. He was so bad-tempered, miserable, sarcastic — what had happened to the gentle, kind boy she had known? She was almost afraid of him. "Come on, Robert, get your pyjamas on quickly and then you won't be cold, will you? You'll freeze if you stand about like that."

"But it's my bathtime now," said Robert.

"No bath tonight," said Victoria. "Straight to bed. *Bed*, Stella." Perhaps she should bath them, perhaps they needed it, but she simply couldn't face it. They couldn't be *that* dirty.

"*Teddy* wants a bath," grumbled Robert as she lifted him up to the top bunk. "Teddy's dirty. Oh, dear."

"Oh dear, indeed," said Victoria, giving him a quick peck on the cheek. She would quite have liked to hug him, but that would have been idiotic. The last thing she ought to do was to get fond of him. She'd never see him again.

"That was quick," said Daniel, without looking away from the television. "Haven't they had a bath?"

"Won't hurt them, just for once," said Victoria, nervously.

"I didn't hear you go to the bathroom — haven't you even given them a wash? Oh, Jesus Christ." He stood up. "I'm not having my kids going to bed dirty. *I'll* wash them. You just sit down. You're the one who's been out working all day to keep us, after all. It's only fair that I should wash the kids. Christ!"

Victoria sat down in the armchair and gazed sightlessly at the flickering images on the TV screen. There was nothing she could do. And suddenly she was no longer afraid, but angry. Who was

128

Daniel to speak to her in this way? He was treating her like a subordinate, an underling. Not a single word of sympathy for her illness, which was genuine for all *he* knew . . . well, he wasn't going to work his frustrations out on *her*.

"About dinner," she said coldly, when he returned, some ten minutes later. "We might as well get something from that takeaway around the corner. Chicken and sweetcorn, or . . ."

"At their prices? Do you know how much they charge for a small bag of *chips*? I don't know what's come over you, Victoria. We're a week behind with the rent, for God's sake, and you want to splash out on takeaway meals just because you've got a bit of a headache? Well, if you're too ill to cook you're certainly too ill to eat. I'll get myself a sandwich."

"Fine," said Victoria. Daniel glared at her.

"My mother," he said, "never failed, never once failed to have a hot meal ready for us in the evenings. My father never had to come home and make himself a sandwich. You're turning out exactly like your mother."

"And what do you mean by that?"

"Oh, come on. I visited your home often enough. It was a pigsty. You said so yourself. Dirty dishes, coffee cups everywhere, dust inches thick — the carpet would have fainted at the sight of a hoover. It's not good enough, Victoria. I'm out all day working. You've got nothing to do except keep an eye on the kids, you've got the whole day, and this place is a wreck. I always have to remind you before you do anything, and now there's no *dinner* . . ."

"You try staying at home all day with the kids! You think it's a doddle? It's bloody tiring. And it's boring! Ever tried holding a stimulating conversation with Stella? You're virtually the only adult I've spoken to all day, and you haven't had a pleasant word to say since you came in!"

"Don't swear," said Daniel. "You know I don't like it." He went over to the kitchen, and started slicing bread. I see, thought Victoria, you can say "Jesus Christ" but I can't say "bloody". So much for equality. Daniel returned with his sandwiches, and two cups of coffee. "Thanks," said Victoria surprised. The gesture took some of the edge off her crossness. She hadn't really had such a hard day; after the first couple of hours she'd scarcely done a thing. And it *was* rotten for Daniel to have to come home and do things like this; she couldn't really blame him for being a bit put out. It was just that all the things he was saying, and the way he was saying them, were so offensive, so irritating. The problem obviously was that he was working at a job way below his capabilities. She would have to see to it that he got that degree.

Daniel ate one sandwich before he spoke. "All right," he said. "Maybe you don't have the most exciting life in the world. I understand that. But you must have known how it would be. And I do think that if you put more effort into things, you'd get more pleasure out of them. You've seemed so much more contented lately; you were really settling down and devoting yourself to being a good wife and mother" — "aaargh!" thought Victoria — "and now here you are again, complaining, moaning, messing around like you did in the beginning. I thought you'd got over that."

"Well — things get on top of me sometimes," said Victoria. She didn't like what she was hearing. "It would have been so much better all round, wouldn't it, if we didn't have the children, if I could go out to work too — and there'd be piles more money . . ."

"Oh, I'd never allow my wife to work," said Daniel, and Victoria gaped. She had heard that before — his father had said it. But surely Daniel was nothing like his father? And then she remembered the drab clothes in the wardrobe . . . "he thinks women only wear bright clothes to attract men . . ."

"But, Daniel," she said, "surely in this day and age that's a bit ridiculous. Woman don't *want* . . ."

"Look, Victoria, maybe we are near the end of the twentieth century, but basic truths about human beings don't change. Men go out to work to keep their families, and no self-respecting man should tolerate anything else. I'm not saying men and women aren't equal — they're just different. Woman are designed for homemaking, and that's how it's been since the year dot. It's different for single women; obviously they must work. They have to live. But marriage changes everything. And I can't imagine why women should complain; they get by far the best of it.

130

Someone to look after them, to take the responsibility off their shoulders, to provide for them . . . they need never do another day's work . . ."

"Housework is work," said Victoria. "Children are work. What makes you think otherwise? And what if that pretty little list happens to be the last thing a woman wants? What if she *wants* responsibility?"

"Women aren't like that," said Daniel, devouring the last sandwich in a crumby mouthful.

"Well, I think . . ."

"Victoria, you don't have to think. I know I'm right."

"Oh yes — that's what it comes down to, isn't it? That's what you really think about women. When they marry they forfeit not only their right to financial independence, but also the right to have *opinions*. To have an independent *brain*."

"I wish you wouldn't talk like that, Victoria. It's not a question of having opinions — of course everyone's entitled to opinions — but yes, I do think that as my wife you should have some respect for me as the head of the family . . ."

"As a *man*, you mean. Well, let me tell you, respect isn't something that's the birthright of the male sex. And what do you mean, head of the family? We're equal partners in this, Daniel. I'm the head of the family as much as you are." Oh, this was foolish; arguing would get her nowhere . . . but she *couldn't* hold her tongue. Nobody had ever bulldozed Victoria Hadley into acquiescence.

"You really must be ill, Victoria. You've never spoken to me like this before."

"Then I should have," she said, more alarmed than ever at the thought of the future Victoria meekly agreeing; yes, Daniel, you're the head of the family, you make all the decisions, I'm just a poor feeble thing, you tell me what I should think, while I fulfil myself by peeling the potatoes. Daniel was shaking his head in disbelief, but said nothing; either he'd worked off the irritation built up during the day, or, more likely, he thought she was having a temporary brainstorm and would be best left alone to get on with it.

There followed a period of tranquillity, of coffee-sipping and

131

television-watching, and Victoria began, slowly, gradually, to relax. It was past eight already; Daniel seemed to have got over his bad temper; she had survived the storm, and in half an hour she might, reasonably, go to bed. She'd had nothing to eat since the cheese on toast at lunchtime, but she didn't seem to be hungry. Yes — she'd have an early night, and the clock would whisk her back, and then in the safety, the familiarity of summer 1983, she could calmly think things through. There was much to think about. Daniel seemed to have grown up to hold all his father's views, views with which she could never agree, to which she could never submit . . . and yet, she *had*. The future Victoria was emerging as someone who had given up, somewhere along the way. Someone who now allowed herself to be dominated totally. Victoria could not relate this to herself. The future Mrs Priestley seemed to be going the way of Mrs Priestley senior. It was frightening. And then, the bombshell exploded. Daniel said, casually:

"Where did you put my trousers?"

"Which trousers?" Victoria felt herself tensing, tightening inside, as if a large hand were ungently fashioning an intestinal helter skelter out of her gut.

"The ones you picked up from the cleaners. My brown ones. I don't see them in the wardrobe."

"I'm sorry, Daniel. I forgot." She knew it wouldn't be good enough.

"You forgot?" said Daniel, uncoiling in his chair like a cobra preparing for a kill. "Pardon me, Victoria, but didn't you walk past there four times today? It must have taken an enormous effort of will to forget. It must have taken fantastic self-control on your part to walk past four times, and not to go in. Really you're to be congratulated on your strength of character. I don't . . ."

"Oh, quit that infantile sarcasm," snapped Victoria. "I forgot, that's all, I just forgot. You don't need to write a novel about it. You've got loads of trousers in the wardrobe."

"Most of which, as you well know, don't fit me any more. I particularly wanted those trousers for tomorrow. It's the one thing I asked you to do today — all day you've got to sit around feeling sorry for yourself, and you couldn't be bothered, you couldn't *remember* to do one small thing for me, while I'm out working to keep us . . ."

"Oh, shut up! Can't you hear what you sound like? That's about six times you've said that. You're like a bloody parrot." The words seemed to be speaking themselves, to be emerging quite independently of Victoria. She didn't want to shout at him — she wanted them to be friends, to be happy — oh, but she couldn't stand the way he was going on.

"You really must be ill," Daniel said, coldly. He'd said that before, as well.

"At least I'm not ill in the *brain*," Victoria said, despite herself, and then shrank back, waiting for his reaction. For a second she really thought he was going to hit her. If he did, she'd scream till the house trembled. But he didn't move. A dark, impenetrable expression came over him, as if a blind had been drawn over his face, and he said:

"Oh, this is all a waste of time. I should never have married you. You're totally unsuitable for marriage. You're impossible to live with."

"Well, you made the decision, so don't complain if you don't like it. It was your choice."

"My choice? Some choice I had. Oh, Daniel, Daniel, I'm pregnant, what shall I do, I'm so frightened . . . I didn't let you down, did I? I got you the address of that nice clinic, you'd have been in and out, end of problem, but oh no, Daniel, I want this baby so badly, I'm so unhappy, Daniel, I can't live with my parents one day longer, I only want to be with you, please don't go back to Cambridge and leave me, we'll be all right together, you know it's what we always wanted, please help me, Daniel. You trapped me! There was no bloody way out! I gave up my chance of a degree, defied my father, gave up my family for you, and I've kept you ever since, working at whatever rubbish job I could get — and you have the nerve to sit there and whine at me that it was my *choice*! You can go to hell." He got up and left the room; the last Victoria heard of him was the slamming of the front door.

Later, when she crawled into bed, for the first time she found cause to be grateful to the future Victoria. In the drawer in the bedside table there were tranquillizers, splendid strong ones just like her mother's, and two different kinds of sleeping pill, the passport to oblivion.

THIRTEEN

"But it's nearly a week now," said Mrs Hadley.

"Mmm," said her husband, gazing with regret at a powdery lump in his Instant Mashed Potato.

"Nobody stays in bed for a week."

"Wish I could," said Mr Hadley. "Good way of conserving energy, in this heat."

Mrs Hadley sighed, and mopped her glistening brow. She did try to glow gracefully, but unfortunately she was genetically programmed to sweat like a pig.

"It's something to do with Daniel, I know it is, but she won't talk about it. Won't tell me a thing. Just that she doesn't want to see him, or speak to him."

"They're always having bust-ups at that age. Different boyfriend every week. Don't know what you're worrying about."

"But — I thought Daniel was different, somehow. And *he* doesn't seem to know about any bust-up. The poor boy's been on the phone, three times a day, begging me to persuade her to talk to him. He's been round here five times. I've never seen anybody look so bewildered."

"Hmm," said Mr Hadley. "It sounds to me as if you'd better stay in with her tonight."

"Oh — what's the point of that? She just stays in her room. It makes no difference if I'm here or not. And I want to play bridge tonight, I'm coming."

"No, you're not. You've played every evening this week, so far.

Can't you stay home with your daughter *once*, when you're supposedly so worried about her?"

"I want to *come* . . ."

"Well, I don't want you to. I'd like a break from you for once. Honestly, Pat, you're like a *leech* . . ."

Victoria could hear every word. They never could remember to keep their voices down when they were arguing. She wasn't actually in her bed, but on it; sprawled out on the cover in a skimpy red sundress. She hadn't planned to stay there for a week, but somehow one day had dragged into another, and there was nothing better to do. If she went out, Daniel might be lurking in the street. And she certainly didn't want to spend a single second with either of her parents. So she might as well stay where she was.

She hadn't once cried. It was as though she were still in shock, still dazed by the enormity of what had happened. And yet, her brain had accepted the truth; that she and Daniel had absolutely no future together — that she must end it now. That their relationship, if pursued, would take just the same disastrous course as had her own parents', or Daniel's parents'. Probably it would combine the worst features of both; that was how it had seemed to be heading. She knew it, but didn't yet feel it. Of one thing she was certain — she mustn't see Daniel. She mustn't allow herself to run the risk that her resolve might be shaken.

She had lost so much. All her plans, her dreams, her happy future, the anticipation of which would have seen her through the miserable present — all gone. All she had left was *this* — this flat, herself, and her parents, quarrelling away next door. The current row had just reached its climax with her father saying coldly that he was leaving now, in the car, on his own, and there was an end to it. Couldn't her mother tell when she wasn't wanted? Slamming of front door. And now there was her mother crying. She cried for ten minutes solid, and then went sniffily to the bathroom. Victoria heard face-washing noises, and then she came out again, opened Victoria's door, and said, with a laughable attempt at normality:

"I'm going to the bridge club, Victoria. I'll be back at the usual time." She looked dreadful. She'd put no make-up on, her eyes were still red from crying, she hadn't even changed out of the crumpled sweaty dress she'd been wearing all day. Victoria turned away. Her mother was like a bad dream.

"Don't go," she said, not even trying to keep the disgust out of her voice. "Don't you realize he doesn't want you there? Why humiliate yourself by tagging along after someone who doesn't want you?"

"Mind your own business!" said her mother sharply.

"Well, at least do something to your face, then. Do you want the whole world to know you've been crying? Haven't you got any pride? Do you want them to be *sorry* for you?"

"Shut up!" screamed her mother. "Shut up, shut up! Why shouldn't they know how he treats me? I don't care!" The door slammed again. Victoria got up. She pulled her travelling bag out of the wardrobe and began to pack. She took a couple of changes of clothes, a nightdress, her savings book, all the money she had — just over twelve pounds — Gran's locket, now empty, and the clock. She went into the bathroom and packed her toothbrush, her Woodland Breeze anti-perspirant, and all the make-up she could squeeze into a sponge-bag. She couldn't live here anymore.

Slowly, slowly in the heat, which was still powerful, heavy and sticky at seven in the evening, she walked down West End Lane, over the bridge and turned in at West Hampstead tube station. The Jubilee Line took her straight through to Charing Cross, where she bought another ticket and heaved her bag wearily over to the indicator board. A train would be leaving in four minutes from platform 2. Victoria went through the gate, had her ticket clipped and found a seat halfway down the train.

The worst of the rush hour was over, but the train was packed nevertheless; sweaty bodies were crammed in all around her, sticking to the seats, fanning themselves with evening papers. And as the train lurched forwards, rolled slowly out of the station, crossed the Thames and crawled into Waterloo before picking up speed for its journey southward, she realized, too late, that she was in a smoking compartment. All the seats were taken now, and if she tried to move, she would have to stand. The combination of heat and fumes made her head swim. The train chugged from station to station, stopping at every one. When at

137

last they arrived at Hambourne, Victoria staggered to the Ladies and was horribly sick. The acid taste of her own vomit burned in her throat; by the time she reached Gran's doorstep, she was about as weak and as miserable as she could ever remember being in her whole life. And Gran opened the door, took one look and straightaway pulled Victoria into her arms. For the first time since the whole mess began, there was someone to take care of things, to make everything all right; so violent was the relief that at last the floodgates opened, and she began to cry all the tears that had been frozen inside her.

"That's been bottled up for some time, I can tell," said Gran, ushering her inside. "I was always a bottler myself. Not your mother, though. With her it was flash floods. Come in, child. It's cool in the living-room. I have one of those splendid oscillating fans which send breezes in every direction. Now, sit down, and tell me what this is all about. No — first a drink. You must be so hot — and you don't look at all well."

"I was sick in the loo at Hambourne station."

"Oh, my dear, how horrid for you. But rather clever, to hold it in for so long. I should probably have been sick on the train, and put all the commuters off their dinner. Now, how about some iced orange juice?" Victoria nodded gratefully, and soon Gran was back with a whole jugful of juice, and two glasses, on a tray.

"I've come to live with you," said Victoria.

"Why?" said Gran, not sounding at all surprised.

"I can't live with *them* any more," said Victoria, in between gulps of juice. She was parched; it tasted like nectar. "Gran, I just can't. You can't imagine what it's like, day after day . . ." and out it all poured. "And God knows what'll happen when they get back tonight — he'll be beastly, and she'll cry and cry — and I've just had to break off with Daniel who was the only thing I cared about in the world — and I can't stand it, Gran. I can't take any more of it."

"Hold on, hold on. Tell me about Daniel. From what you said in all your letters he sounded like a lovely young man. What happened?"

"Oh, it wasn't that anything *happened*." Not even Gran could be told about the clock. She could see that Victoria was in quite a

138

state, and the heat does do funny things to people . . . and then she wouldn't take seriously the other things that Victoria had to tell her. "I just began to see that it wasn't going to work out. I realized that his attitudes, his opinions — woman's place is behind the kitchen sink, squeezing the Fairy Liquid, sort of thing — would make it impossible for us to — you know, have any sort of future. I don't know that it's anyone's fault, particularly — there may be girls that love to be treated like that. But I'm not one of them. I didn't want to believe it, I tried hard not to, to pretend that it would be all right, and he'd change — because I cared about him so much. But it was no good." Half of her was hoping that Gran would wave a wand, and say: 'But you mustn't give up so easily, child! Of course you can change him' . . . but Gran said instead:

"How remarkably mature of you to have seen all that, and been strong enough to act on it. I remember now, it kept coming up in your letters — what a strange man Daniel's father was in his attitudes, and how much Daniel was influenced by him."

"That's right. He would have treated me exactly as his father does his mother — and she's barely a human being, she's been so completely crushed. So I had to break it off now, because the longer I left it, the harder it would have become. Do you see?"

"I see very well. I only wish I'd been so sensible at fifteen, Victoria. My dear, I know how it hurts. I do remember, even after all these years, how it hurts. But of course you know how much more hurt you're saving yourself from, in the long run."

"It's just that he was *all I had* — and things have been so bloody awful at home that I used to sort of mentally escape, by dreaming about the future. And now there's nothing to escape to. So I can't stay there. I can't."

"Are they playing bridge as much as ever?"

"More than ever. Her in particular. She goes along every single evening, now. It was getting on my father's nerves; you could see he wanted to get away on his own. I don't care how much she goes. I was glad to see the back of her."

"Of course you care," said Gran. "You've always cared. Why else would you have behaved so dreadfully these past years? Oh, you were always a naughty, spirited child, and quite right too, but there was a point at which you changed. You became a regular little brat, so I was told."

"That wasn't because I *cared*, it was because I hated them. . ."

"You know better than that, Victoria. You were what — eight or nine? — when your mother began playing bridge so frequently. You felt neglected, not unreasonably, I dare say, and so you began to behave quite appallingly, in order to get their attention. Your mother's mostly, I think. Did you really once put a noose round your neck and pretend you'd hanged yourself? I would have laughed, except that really it was so sad."

"How do you know about that? Did my mother *tell* you?"

"Of course she did. She has phoned me, over the years, you know. She told me all the awful things you did. She also told me that you've been quite different, recently."

"Yes, but not for the reasons *she* thinks, all that blah about how mature and grown up I am all of a sudden. It's because — I've only recently realized what they're like, what they're doing to each other, how hopeless it all is."

"People who haunt bridge clubs," said Gran, "excluding, maybe, professionals, who have a sound financial reason for their presence, are not, as far as I can tell, happy people. Usually there's something very wrong, or lacking, in their lives, and they flock to these clubs to seek oblivion behind thirteen playing cards. That's why I gave up club bridge. I was used to friendly social games, and all the bitterness and frustration I found at the club quite ruined any enjoyment of the game for me."

"Gran! I never knew you were a bridge player. I thought you were above that sort of thing."

"You make it sound like a criminal activity. Where did you think your mother learned it from? It's a very good game. You'd be excellent at it."

"No! One thing I'm never ever going to do is learn bridge. And I'm very glad you don't play any more."

"Oh, but I do. I still enjoy the occasional social game. But, Victoria, the point I'm trying to make is that your mother — I can't speak for your father, and I don't in all honesty care about him, except in as much as he affects you and Pat — your mother has been very unhappy since you were about eight, and all this bridge has been something of an escape, a release for her. It wasn't a rejection of you. She just couldn't help it."

"I know she's been unhappy. And I know why: because my father's had other women, and she's potty about him and he doesn't care about her a bit. I know all that. What I don't know, and I know you *do* know, is what he's been doing with his money all these years. I haven't been able to work that one out."

Gran sighed deeply. "You're so sharp," she said — "so observant." Victoria felt like a fraud; she hadn't noticed a thing, until the heavy contrast of their life in 1976 had forced her into awareness. "I'm so sorry, Victoria dear. These are horrid things for a child to discover — not that you're a child any more. I think it's time you . . . "

The telephone rang, and Gran went out to answer it. Victoria sat back, and kicked her shoes off. She was still in something of a daze; her thoughts seesawed from Daniel to her parents and back again, occasionally diverting to the prospect of living in Hambourne — what would it be like, for someone who had never lived far from central London? This was a very sleepy little place, but perhaps that was just what she needed.

Gran was gone for ages, and when she came back, her face was such a jumble of expressions that Victoria could not begin to guess if the news had been good or bad.

"That was your mother. She came home from the bridge club, and found you weren't there. So she phoned to see if you'd come to me."

"Oh. You did tell her I was staying, didn't you? I won't go back, Gran. I *won't*."

"The conversation didn't exactly go like that. Calm down, Victoria. Let's have some more orange juice, while I tell you what's happened."

"How d'you mean, happened?"

"Well — she wasn't very coherent, but from what I could make out, she arrived at the bridge club tonight to find your father sitting in a quiet corner, his head about two inches away from that of a person called Sheila Everett. As soon as he saw Pat he got up and walked out, with the above-mentioned Ms Everett at his side."

"Sheila *Everett*? I don't believe it. He hates her. He says her bidding would make a certified moron sound like Einstein. He says she does for lay down contracts what Hitler did for Jews. He . . ."

"*That* is in appallingly bad taste," said Gran. "Flippant remarks about the most obscene mass-murderer of the century — jokes about genocide — it shocks me to think you've been exposed to remarks like that. It shocks me."

"But Sheila *Everett*," said Victoria, wishing she'd kept her mouth shut.

"Don't you ever say a thing like that again in my house. All right. We'll say no more about it. Yes — Sheila Everett."

"I always thought she was some feeble old hag."

"Apparently not. Pat's suspected for some time, she said, that something was going on. That's why she's been so very low lately; and of course, that's why she wouldn't have your father going to the club without her."

"Mmm." Victoria was trying to turn her image of Sheila Everett inside out, but it was no good, the name just conjured up an old crone with a hunched back and a walking stick, her hands shaking as she pulled out the only card to give declarer the contract. "So — my father walked out with her, and then what happened?"

"It seems that your mother broke down in hysterics, and some kind person took her home."

"Kind! Huh. I bet they all enjoyed every minute of it. Some drama in their miserable little lives. Some really juicy gossip to feed on."

"Possibly. Anyway — something good has come out of the whole hideous scene. Your mother has finally snapped and seen sense. She's leaving him. I'm so glad I could cheer. I know he's your father, my dear, and perhaps I shouldn't speak this way — but it's no good, he's a cold cruel man and I've always loathed him. The way he's treated my only child — not that she was blameless, I suppose. But I'll come to that in a moment. She's finishing it, Victoria — she's packing a suitcase right now, and she's getting the next train."

"Train? What train?"

"The train here, of course. Where else would she go?"

"But she can't come here! I've only just got away from her! I don't want her here. She'll be crying and howling . . ."

"Yes, I expect she will, but if she can't come and cry to her mother I don't know who she can cry to. Victoria, you mustn't . . ."

"But she doesn't even get on with you! She hardly ever sees you! She snaps whenever I even mention you, she always has . . ."

"If you'd kindly let me get a word in. That is something else that should become clear to you when I've told you my story. I managed to persuade your mother that it's time you knew certain things. Now, do you want to sit there raving and wailing like a three-year-old, or do you want to listen?"

"I'll listen." It was the only way she'd find out anything. "But, Gran, I don't want . . "

"Victoria! One more word from you, and that's the end of this conversation. All right? Good. Now, I'll start right at the beginning, at the time when your parents met." She was speaking as calmly as if this were to be a bedtime story of fairies and goblins. "At the time they were both students, living on grants. They decided to move in together, but all they could afford was a bedsitter — just one room. So they took that." Her voice made it quite clear that she had not approved of this move. "And so when they got married and you came along, they had quite a problem on their hands."

You bet they did. She must have been a strong contender for Unwanted Pregnancy of the Year. "You needn't be so tactful," she said. "I'm afraid I know about that too. You can put things in their proper order."

"Very well. They discovered you were on the way, and they got married — and really there was no way they could have kept a baby in that one room. And neither of them was qualified yet — they were simply in no position to keep you. They couldn't afford to. And your mother would have had to give up her education, she'd never have got her degree . . ."

"I always forget that she's got a degree," said Victoria. "She doesn't behave in any way like somebody should if they've got a degree. Sorry — I didn't mean to interrupt."

"Well — it was decided that it would be best for you to live with me, at least until your father had completed his studies and was in a position to start earning money."

"Oh — so *that's* why . . ."

"Why what?"

Why the house in Fulham had seemed so familiar on her recent visit, she had almost said. Why she'd had all those things there, the high chair, the cot, and that lovely room. It hadn't felt like a holiday, somehow . . .

"I have these memories," she said. "I could remember this house with a big boiler in the kitchen that made funny noises, and an apple tree in the garden . . . but my mother said I couldn't possibly remember." And suddenly it was what her mother *hadn't* said that was significant. "But, Gran, she never told me! She's never ever told me that I lived with you when I was a baby. Why does she lie to me? Why pretend? What difference does it make to her?"

"Well, because of the way she felt about it, it made a lot of difference. You see, because you came straight to me — I took you home from the hospital — she never had a chance to form any sort of bond with you. She used to visit, of course, two or three times a week, but it wasn't the same. Really I suppose you thought of me as your mother. And when the time came for her to take you away, you went berserk. You screamed and kicked and howled, you pushed her away — it was a very distressing scene — and she felt very badly about it. She did give birth to you, after all." Victoria winced at the thought of it. "And it turned her against me. Partly jealousy, and partly guilt, I suspect, at having left you with me for so long. You were over eighteen months, by then. And she wouldn't let me see you; she wouldn't talk to you about me. That's actually why I moved down here. The house in Fulham seemed so empty, when you'd gone."

"I'm sorry," Victoria said, after a moment. "It must have been much worse for you than it was for anyone else."

"I suppose I stupidly — and wrongly — hoped that they might leave you with me for ever. Your father, you see, he showed no interest in you . . ."

144

"They should have! She had no right to take me away just because she felt guilty and jealous! She never wanted a child at all! She didn't have any claim to me . . ."

"Victoria, you must see that she did. She's your mother."

"No she didn't, and I'll tell you why! Because the only reason she ever had a bloody baby at all was to get my father to marry her! Because she knew he was the sort of man who'd do that — even if she didn't know how he'd make her suffer for it — and there was no other way she could get him! To her I was just a thing she was using, not a person at all." She knew it was the truth. She had heard the same story a week before, she realized with an overwhelming sense of horror and shame. Patterns repeating themselves.

"Victoria, neither you nor I can ever possibly know that," said Gran, firmly. "And I want to hear you promise me that you will never, not even in twenty years' time, say anything like that to your mother. Do you promise?"

"All right," said Victoria. It had been said once; it needn't be said again.

"What I was trying to get round to is this: your relationship with your mother didn't get off to a very good start. Of course, you didn't understand; you were only a little mite. And what you clearly still don't understand is that she's very fond of you. The problem has always been that she was fonder of your father. It wasn't that she didn't love you. She was just so unhappy; it was hard for her to show it. Anyway, now at least she's made a break. Things can only get better."

"Why . . . oh. Yes." Victoria had actually forgotten that her mother was, at this very moment, leaving her father. Well, it wasn't really going to change a thing. It was all too late. The only difference would be that probably from now on she would hate her father more than she did her mother.

"I never want to see my father again," she said. "I'm ashamed to be related to him."

"I'm glad you've stopped lumping them together as 'my parents' every time you speak," Gran said drily. "Not, as I said earlier, that your mother's blameless. She should have ended it years ago. But I forget — you still don't know it all."

"Then tell me."

"This is much the hardest thing yet. But it will be better for you, and for your mother, if I tell you. She's going to need all your support in the months ahead." Victoria opened her mouth, but Gran went smoothly on. "About eight years ago, your father had an affair with his secretary, a girl called Philippa Wright. She wasn't the first, but she was the first that your mother found out about, and also the first to get pregnant. She wanted your father to leave Pat and marry her, which he refused to do; but he did feel responsible for her, and he's been supporting her, and the child, ever since. I'm sorry, Victoria. I know this must come as a dreadful shock. But now you understand why there hasn't been much money. He couldn't afford to keep on that house you had, and that was why you moved to a much smaller flat. And — that's why your mother changed so much at that time."

"I understand," said Victoria. She wondered why she could summon up no feelings of loathing towards this Philippa who had caused so much upheaval and misery. All she could feel was pity. Just a daft little thing, probably, who'd had a wild crush on her boss, and thought he was going to marry her — and she'd ended up with no job, no boss, and an illegitimate child to bring up all on her own. The child — in a way, that was the hardest thing to grasp. All these years she'd thought of herself as an only child, while in fact she had a little half-brother or sister — six years old, now. "Yes. Now I see it all. It was the one thng that never crossed my mind, and even if it had, how could I have believed it? I couldn't believe that my mother would stick with him after that; allow her nice house to be sold, so that he could keep a stupid girl . . . nobody could believe that."

"I won't tell you what my reaction was," said Gran, who was looking more relaxed all of a sudden — relieved, probably, that she'd taken it so well. "I do remember smashing a very nice vase, and wishing I had Pat's head here to smash it against, rather than the wall, which hadn't offended me in any way. But, Victoria — don't be too hard on her. She's been through enough, and she's got a bad time ahead of her. We really must help her all we can."

Victoria didn't like that 'we'. "I can't help her. I've got enough problems of my own, without her on my back. And she won't be staying, will she? You can't possibly want both of us living here."

"Neither of you will be living here," Gran said.

"What do you mean? You can't turn me away! And there's nowhere to go — I'm not going back to the flat with *him* there . . ."

"Your father has always said that he'd move out if Pat wanted him to. He's the one who'll be leaving the flat. Pat's just getting out of the way for a week or so while he moves out. However long it takes."

"He can't afford to run *three* households. It's not possible."

"Well, why should he? Your mother can go back to work."

"You try telling her that."

"Oh, I shall be telling her, don't worry." Her tone left little room for doubt. Victoria's mother would do as she was told. "There's nothing like work for seeing someone through a crisis. Sitting around and thinking about it is the worst possible thing."

"Well, I don't want to live with her. Have you seen the way she keeps the place? It's filthy. It's a mess. It's . . ."

"Really, Victoria, if you feel so strongly about it, it shouldn't be beyond you to apply yourself with a duster and a vacuum cleaner for half an hour a day. I never heard such nonsense. Of course you must go back and live with her. You're doing seven O Levels next year, yes? Do you think it's easy to switch schools in your final year? They're probably doing a completely different syllabus down here." Her voice softened at the transparent misery in Victoria's expression. "Come, child, it's not so bad. You're more than welcome to spend the rest of the holidays with me. I'm sure the break will do you good. But then, back to London with you. Your mother's a lot more unhappy than you are, whatever you may think, and you can help her. You're so much stronger than she is, my dear. You're the tough one."

Victoria hadn't thought about school. It would, certainly, be an incredible drag, starting somewhere else. And she'd never find another Lesley. But there would be Sophie, too: a constant reminder. "Daniel," she said. "I wanted to get right away from all that."

"Daniel is going to Cambridge in October. A little distance is

147

worth a ton of coldness, when it comes to ending a thing of that kind. Out of sight, out of mind."

"Absence makes the heart grow fonder," snapped Victoria, who wasn't about to be out-proverbed by anyone. "And I'm not strong. I don't know why you should think that. If I were so strong I wouldn't have had to come here. I'd have coped with it all on my own. Well, I couldn't. Gran, you're all I've got to fall back on. Can't you see that?"

"No," said Gran. "I see something quite different. You've got something much better than me; you've got you. You're going back to St. Catherine's, and you'll get your A Levels, and go off to do Biology, just as you always wanted, and maybe you'll meet the right person to settle down with, and maybe you won't. But it won't matter, because you'll still be you."

"Oh, I shan't get married, not ever," said Victoria. "That's something I know. Marriage is a disaster."

"Don't be too sure. I don't like to brag about it, but if you'd known your grandfather I don't think you'd have said our marriage was a disaster. The memories of it have given me happiness all these years, and I've no need of rose-coloured glasses; my vision is quite clear. That's why I'm glad for you that your brief time with Daniel was so happy. It wasn't wasted. Not only did you learn from it, but you'll be able to look back on it with pleasure in years to come. Nobody can ever take that from you."

Yes. She could look back; and she could do more than that. If she set the clock, she could *go* back — relive the Daniel days, any time she wanted. And if, once more, she set it for twenty-three, presumably it would take her forward into something quite different, now that she had ruled out the Daniel-future. But she wasn't going to travel forward again. Not ever.

She knew the immediate future, in any case. She could see now that she would have to go back and live with her mother for a couple of years. But her mother, on her own, could not be nearly so bad as her mother with her father. She'd have nobody to have bridge arguments with; she wouldn't even be able to *go* to the bridge club, for fear of bumping into Sheila Everett, and *him*. No bridge, and a full-time job again — she might even become a normal person. Victoria thought she could put up with it, during term-time, anyway. And in the holidays she would come to Hambourne and Gran.

As for the clock, the best thing she could do with it would be to put it aside for a few years, while she studied science. Maybe she wouldn't do Biology after all; she'd do Physics, instead. Eventually she was going to find out how the thing worked. It might take a very long time, but she'd find out. There was always a logical explanation for everything. Of course, in the meantime, she *could* go back to visit Daniel, if she got lonely. But she didn't think she ever would. It wasn't any good, living on memories of other people. What Gran had said was true. There was only yourself, in the end.

And then the doorbell rang, and Gran got up to let her mother in.

K. M. Peyton

THE PLAN FOR
BIRDSMARSH

Illustrated by
VICTOR G. AMBRUS

Oxford   Toronto   Melbourne
OXFORD UNIVERSITY PRESS
1979

Oxford University Press, Walton Street, Oxford OX2 6DP

OXFORD LONDON GLASGOW
NEW YORK TORONTO MELBOURNE WELLINGTON
KUALA LUMPUR SINGAPORE JAKARTA HONG KONG TOKYO
DELHI BOMBAY CALCUTTA MADRAS KARACHI
NAIROBI DAR ES SALAAM CAPE TOWN

© K. M. Peyton 1965

First published 1965

First issued in New Oxford Library 1979

To Chris, John, Roger
and Michele

Author's note
With apologies to the village of Bradwell which, for
the purpose of this story, has been obliterated from the
map, power-station and all, and replaced by the entirely
fictitious village of Birdsmarsh with its entirely
fictitious inhabitants.

British Library Cataloguing in Publication Data

Peyton, K. M.
The plan for Birdsmarsh. – (New Oxford library).
I. Title   II. Series
823'.9'1J   PZ7.P4483
ISBN 0-19-277096-9

*Printed and bound in Great Britain by
Morrison & Gibb Ltd, London and Edinburgh*

I

THE VISITOR

'Paul!'

Gus stuck his head up over the sea-wall and looked down on his friend's old smack where she lay wedged in the outfall. A plume of smoke drifted from her rusted tin chimney and the plank was in place from the muddy salting to the deck, so he knew Paul was on board.

'Putting that old bird together, I bet,' Gus muttered. He had come to tinker with the engine, which would annoy Paul. Paul Fairfax looked on his smack as a workshop. The fact that it was a boat was entirely coincidence as far as he was concerned, but to Gus, fisherman's son, she was MN 32, built by Aldous of Brightlingsea in 1910, familiarly known as *Swannie* (short for *Swansong*), and deserved better than mouldering in a mud-berth for Paul's benefit. She was old, but she would sail well enough with new rigging and sails. Gus was contriving her rebirth. Paul, dreamy, daft Paul, would have to be persuaded.

'Hi, Gus.' Paul looked up from the cabin table, which was strewn with the bones of a Great Northern diver. He was re-assembling the skeleton with fuse wire and glue, a task which Gus considered impossible and about which Paul himself was beginning to have doubts. He rolled the dried glue off his fore-finger and looked pointedly at the can of petrol Gus had put down on the floor.

'What's that for?'

'I thought I'd have a go at getting the engine started. It's bad for it, never having a run. The tide's nearly up,' Gus said, non-committally.

'Polluting the atmosphere, you lout,' Paul said, but quite cheerfully. 'All you think about.'

'It won't pollute it any worse than that stinking glue you've got there,' Gus pointed out.

Paul stared thoughtfully at the fragmented diver, and sighed. His plan was not turning out a success, just as everyone else but himself had foreseen. He had found the diver's body on the sea-wall, limp and still beautiful, even in death, and he had wanted to perpetuate the poor bird for its trouble, so that it would not have made the journey from the Arctic lakes in vain. It looked as if its remains would now have to be content with committal to the deep. Bones floated, Paul thought. He would wait till the tide was ebbing, so that they would go out to sea where they belonged, not up to Maldon like a little convoy of day-trippers.

'It's a right mess, isn't it?' Gus said, squeezing in round the table to sit by the stove.

'Yes. Hopeless.'

'I was talking to Sydney just now,' Gus continued, in the tone of one getting down to business. 'He said he'd come along later and check *Swannie*'s measurements for sails. He says he'll be able to get us a suit, with a bit of luck.'

'What for?' said Paul.

'Well, you know how keen he is to see her sailing again.' Even as he said it, Gus knew that Paul would not be taken in by this remark. He grinned as Paul gave a sarcastic snort.